MURDER
in *Velvet*

For my mum and dad

- SW

This edition published in 2024
First published in Great Britain 2023
by New Frontier Publishing Europe Ltd
Vicarage House, 58-60 Kensington Church Street, London W8 4DB
www.newfrontierpublishing.co.uk

978-1-915167-56-9 (PB) • 978-1-916790-22-3 (eBook)

Text © 2023 Sarah Wynne
Illustration © 2023 Laura Barrett
Endpapers © 2023 Vector Tradition/Adobe Stock
All rights reserved.

The rights of the author and illustrator have been asserted.

This book is sold subject to the condition that it shall not, by way of trade
or otherwise, be lent, hired out or otherwise circulated in any form of binding or
cover other than that in which it is published. No part of this publication may be
reproduced, stored in a retrieval system, or transmitted, in any form or by any means
(electronic, mechanical, photocopying, recording or otherwise), without the prior
written permission of New Frontier Publishing Europe Ltd.

A CIP catalogue record for this book
is available from the British Library.

Edited by Tasha Evans • Designed by Verity Clark

Printed and bound in Turkey
3 5 7 9 10 8 6 4 2

MURDER
in *Velvet*

SARAH WYNNE

ILLUSTRATED BY LAURA BARRETT

NEW FRONTIER PUBLISHING

CHAPTER 1

For the millionth time, Grace tugged the cuff of her coat down to her wrist. And, for the millionth time, it sprang straight back up, leaving a big chunk of skin exposed. She fingered the threadbare fabric and sighed. It was definitely time for a new coat.

'Mum?' she called as she hurried down the stairs. 'Muuum!'

'In here!'

Grace groaned. She was in her office. Again. Ever

since her boss had hinted at a promotion if she did well at some meeting or other, her mum had practically lived in her office. And if the last few weeks were anything to go by, her mum would *never* listen to her if she was working. Taking a deep breath, Grace pulled open the office door.

As usual, her mum was sitting behind the large mahogany desk, frowning at a document in her hands.

'Mum? Can I buy a new coat? This one's too small – it doesn't even cover my wrists any more.' Grace stepped inside and held up her arms. The dark grey woollen material obligingly rode up her arms.

'It's fine,' her mother replied, highlighting a passage on the page in front of her and not even looking up.

'But Mum, it's for age 11 and I'm 13. *And* it's not just the sleeves that are the problem. If I do it up, I look like a badly stuffed sausage!' she complained, forcing the buttons through the holes and turning on the spot so her mum could take in the full horror of the coat.

'Don't exaggerate, Grace. It's fine for this winter – you can have a new one next year.' Her mum continued to scribble notes and *still* hadn't bothered to look at her.

'*That's* what you said last year!'

With a sigh, her mum put the papers down. She took off her glasses and rubbed at the bridge of her nose. 'Yes, because it was okay last year, and it's still okay this year. Now, you can see I'm busy getting ready for the conference in Edinburgh next weekend …' She gestured at the chaos on her desk.

'But–'

'But nothing, Grace. The roof repairs cost thousands and my car's in for an MOT next week, so we don't have the money for new coats. Maybe, if you let me focus on getting ready for my presentation, I might be in line for the promotion I was telling you about. And if I get that, you can have all the new coats you want,' she said, thrusting her glasses back on and pointedly looking back at the paperwork.

'Argh!' Grace flew out of the room, deliberately leaving the office door open behind her.

'Close the door!' her mum yelled after her, but it was too late – she was already at the top of the stairs.

Grace slammed her bedroom door and flung herself on the bed. It wasn't fair! Of course it wouldn't be okay until next year! But no, Mum was too interested in her work. As usual. Angrily, she groped around under the bed until her fingertips brushed against the object she was looking for. Then, she gently lifted the small trinket box from its hiding place and placed it on the bed next to her.

Inside was a small pile of banknotes and a folded newspaper cutting. Grace pulled out the newspaper and carefully unfolded it. From the moment she'd seen the advert two years ago, she'd started saving every penny she could in order to pay for the annual summer art residential and only needed another £20. Sighing, she pulled out the money and fingered the notes unhappily. If she took money to buy a coat, it could jeopardise her chance of going to the camp. But if she *didn't* buy a new coat, she wouldn't be able to show her face in school. There really was no other choice. Reluctantly, she unfurled three notes from the small bundle and tucked them into the back pocket of her school trousers before replacing the lid and returning the box to its hiding place.

Grace took one last look in the full-length mirror on her wardrobe, sighed and left her bedroom.

Ding Dong! Tap! Tap! Tap!

Grace ran down the remaining stairs and grabbed her backpack from the peg at the bottom. 'I'm going to school now, Mum!' she yelled and pulled open the front door. On the doorstep stood her best friend, Suzy, her pink curls even wilder than usual in the breezy autumn morning.

'Whoa, Grace. What're you *wearing*?'

'Don't even ask,' Grace muttered, checking for her key and slamming the door behind her.

'Well?' her friend prompted as they walked down the path.

'I know, I know! Try telling Mum it doesn't fit – she reckons I'll get another year out of it!'

Suzy snorted with laughter, and Grace couldn't help but smile as she shoulder-barged her friend. 'It's not a laughing matter, Suze! I can't be seen at school in this!'

'Well, it's not your best look. Try undoing the buttons,' her friend suggested.

Grace undid the straining buttons and shivered as the morning chill rushed in. 'Better?' she asked through chattering teeth.

'Not really, but you might freeze to death before you get to school. Problem solved!'

'Helpful, Suze. Really helpful!'

They continued down the tree-lined street of bay fronted terraced houses in companionable silence until they reached the main road at the end of Grace's street.

'Fancy a hot chocolate? We can go to Flava – it's normally open by now,' Suzy asked.

'Hot chocolate? For *breakfast*?'

Suzy grinned. 'You know me – sweet tooth! Come on.' She pulled Grace right at the junction towards the main row of high street shops. The road here was starting to get busy, with people rushing to school or work, or setting up their shops for the day. As they walked past the florist, Flower Power, Grace's next-door neighbour bustled outside, her arms laden with brightly coloured tulips.

'Morning, girls,' she greeted them.

'Morning, Mrs Peel. Do you want a hand with those flowers?' Grace asked as several of the bunches on top tottered precariously.

'I'm fine thanks, love. But– oh!' Mrs Peel staggered as her toe caught on an uneven paving stone, and Grace jumped forwards, catching a large bunch of yellow tulips before they hit the ground. 'Ah, maybe I did need a bit of help!' Mrs Peel smiled at Grace before lowering the flowers into a water-filled bucket in front of the shop. 'Now, did I overhear you girls talking about going to Flava?'

Suzy nodded, smiling at Grace.

'Ah, I'd love a cuppa. The dog managed to get out of the back garden again this morning, the little devil. I spent ages tracking him down and missed my morning tea. I'm parched, but there's no way I'll have time to get a drink with all this stock to get out – you'd be saving my life!'

Scruff, Mrs Peel's Jack Russell, was always getting

into mischief. If he wasn't escaping, he was chewing the sofa or climbing in bins. Only last week, Grace's mum had found him with his head stuck inside a chicken carcass she'd thrown out after Sunday lunch.

'Course we can, Mrs P.' Grace smiled.

'Great. My bag's just inside the door – grab a couple of quid for the tea and a couple for yourselves.'

'Thanks!' Suzy said, taking the money, and the pair hurried on down the road. They soon reached Flava – a tiny building with just enough room inside for a counter and a row of gleaming chrome drinks machines.

'Sure you don't want anything?' Suzy asked as she pulled open the door and inhaled the aroma of freshly brewed coffee.

Grace eyed the queue inside the coffee shop.

'Nah, I'm good. I'll just wait out here.'

Grace placed her backpack on the pavement and had just perched on the windowsill of the coffee shop when a movement outside the charity shop opposite caught her eye.

An old lady had arrived and was pulling open the metal shutters which covered the front. Slowly, the shop sign was revealed. Give and Take. Then, she wheeled out an old sky-blue bicycle, its wicker basket filled with various knick-knacks. She leant it against the storefront and reached into the shop once more to drag out a large blackboard.

CLOSING DOWN SALE. FINAL DAY. EVERYTHING MUST GO! was written in large white letters across it. Her heart lifted. Maybe …

Grace opened the door of the coffee shop.

'Suze, the shop over the road's got a sale on. I'm just going to take a look and see if they've got any coats!' she called.

Suzy gave a thumbs up, and Grace glanced left and right before darting across the road and into the charity shop.

It took a moment for her eyes to adjust to the dim interior after the bright sunshine outside. When they did, the first thing that struck her was the clutter. Clothes covered every surface. Those that weren't folded on shelves or hung on racks were stacked in piles on the floor. Then there was the smell. The musky odour of old clothes filled the air, and Grace was tempted to walk straight out again.

But she *needed* a coat.

Weaving between the towering stacks of old clothes, she made her way to the back wall of the shop where the rails of coats were displayed.

'Wow! For a moment back there, I thought I was going to be buried under a pile of clothes, never to be seen again!' Suzy joked as she joined Grace at the racks. 'Right. Let's get some on you; we've only got a few minutes.' She began to flick through the hangers before pulling out a padded black jacket. 'Here, try this on.'

Grace shrugged off her coat and pulled it on.

'Nope. Next!' her friend said, thrusting another coat at her.

She tried coat after coat after coat. Too tight, too baggy, arms too long, arms too short – nothing was quite right.

'I guess that's it then,' Grace sighed, passing the

last coat back to Suzy. 'Time to face the humiliation at school.'

'Well, you tried. We can go shopping after school if you like,' Suzy replied as they negotiated their way back to the front of the shop. Just as Grace's fingers wrapped around the door handle, a flash of dark green fabric in the window caught her eye.

'Hang on a sec,' she muttered as she took a step closer. It was buried at the bottom of a stack of clothes, and Grace carefully pulled away an assortment of items until she reached the bottom. Gently, she lifted the material and shook it out to see exactly what it was. It was the most beautiful coat she'd ever seen.

'Wow,' Suzy breathed from behind her. 'Try it on.'

Grace slid her arms into the silk-lined sleeves and shrugged it over her shoulders. She turned to her friend, who was strangely quiet for once.

'What? Is it awful?' Grace asked.

Suzy shook her head. 'Look.' She led Grace to a full-length mirror that leant against one of the rails.

It was perfect.

The rich, dark green velvet accentuated the natural copper highlights in her long dark hair. She fastened the three large buttons that ran down the centre and adjusted the collar before turning this way and that to view the coat from every possible angle. She couldn't take her eyes off her reflection. Gently, she ran her fingers over the soft fabric, marvelling at the way it hugged her waist before flaring out to just above her knee. It could have been made for her.

'You have *got* to get it. How much is it?' Suzy asked.

Grace's heart plummeted. It hadn't been on the sale rack – there was no way she'd be able to afford a coat like this. Why had she even tried it on?

Reluctantly, she removed the coat.

'You look, Suze. I can't do it.' She passed the coat to her friend who immediately rifled around inside it.

'Wow, this was made in 1968. Look – it was made by Goldburgh and Sons, Fine Couturiers.' She held the label towards Grace. 'It must have been made especially for someone.'

'But is there a price?'

'Hang on … aha! Here it is.' She held the tag towards the window, unable to make out the digits in the gloom. 'OMG. It's £9.99. You've got to get it!'

Grace grabbed the jacket and squinted at the label herself. There it was, written neatly in black biro. £9.99. She grinned at her friend and dashed over to the counter to pay.

'It's beautiful, isn't it?' the grey-haired lady said as she put the purchase through the till. 'It was only dropped off yesterday, along with the bike outside. I'd just priced it up ready to go on the racks, but you've saved me a job.' She smiled as she carefully folded it into a carrier bag.

'Thank you so much!' Grace said, clutching the bag to her chest, barely able to believe it was really hers.

'Now, you'll be late for school if you don't get a move on.'

School! She'd forgotten all about it!

She hurried out of the shop to where Suzy was finishing the last of her hot chocolate on the pavement outside.

'Come on! We're going to be so dead when we get to school!' Grace laughed as they sprinted down the street.

'Yeah,' Suzy giggled. 'But what a coat!'

CHAPTER 2

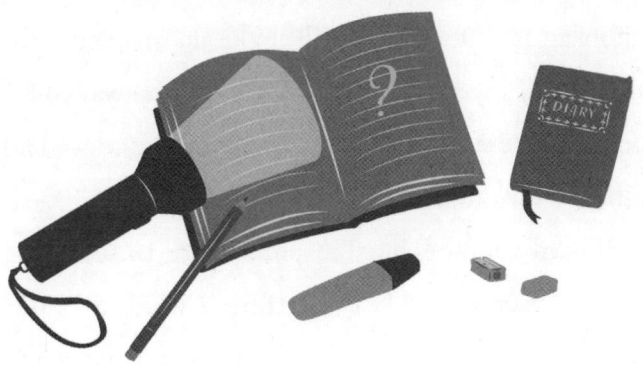

The heavy oak doors to the school were closed when they finally arrived. Never a good sign.

Grace and Suzy glanced anxiously at each other before pushing them open. As expected, the long central corridor was empty. The only indication there was anyone at all in the building was the low murmur of learning that seeped through the dozens of doors that ran either side. There was no way they were going to be able to sneak into class unnoticed.

'Blast it!' Suzy cursed. 'Beany's going to have my head for this!'

'Sorry, it's my fault – I should've waited until after school to look for a coat. I'll make up an excuse for you. I'll say my alarm didn't go off and you waited for me ... or there was a flood in the kitchen and we had to help Mum clean it up.'

'Thanks Grace, but I'm pretty sure I used some of those excuses the last five times I was late.' Suzy shrugged. 'Oh well. Come on, let's just get it over with.'

Brightly coloured banners hung across the corridor advertising the end of term ball. The bulletin boards that lined the walls were covered in notices for clubs, bands seeking members and school news. But as they walked reluctantly down the corridor, Grace's eyes were fixed on only one thing. The door signed 'Office' at the very end.

Grace's heart did cartwheels in her chest as they drew nearer. She'd never had to see the administrator before. Still, she knew from Suzy's tales following her many, many visits that it wouldn't be a pleasant experience. She wiped her clammy palms on her school trousers as they reached the door and knocked.

'Enter!' came the clipped reply.

'I'll go first, take some of the heat away from you,' Grace whispered before pushing open the door.

'Name!' Mrs Beanscough barked, fixing Grace with a steely stare as soon as she entered the room.

'G … Grace Yi, Mrs Beanscough. I'm sorry I'm la–'

'Ah, Miss Yi,' Mrs Beanscough interrupted. 'So glad you finally decided to show your face. You've had something *incredibly* important to attend to this morning I take it?' The school administrator peered at Grace over her half-moon glasses, her pencilled-on eyebrows raised.

Grace opened her mouth to respond but was immediately silenced by a raised palm.

'Don't say a word, young lady. I called your mother when you failed to show for registration, so I know there was no emergency – no cat up a tree or sick aunt.' She paused as she scribbled on a piece of card, and Grace flicked a quick glance at Suzy through the window in the office door.

'Take this.' She thrust the card at Grace.

LATE. LUNCHTIME DETENTION. ONE HOUR was printed across it.

'But ... but that's my whole lunch!' Grace gasped.

'You should have thought of that before turning up twenty minutes after registration. Now get to class.' Mrs Beanscough pointed at the door with a scarlet-painted fingernail, a smirk tugging up one corner of her thin lips.

Grace turned on her heel and strode out of the room.

'And send Miss Blake in!'

Grace shook her head at Suzy as she walked past and mouthed good luck. Suzy grimaced back and went in. As the door slowly swung closed behind her, Grace could just make out the administrator's voice.

'What a surprise, Miss Blake. You're late. Again. And this time with pink hair, no less. I wasn't aware that pink was considered a natural hair colour, as specified in the school uniform policy.' Mrs Beanscough paused. 'Now, what shall we do to encourage you to arrive at school on time and stop breaking the rules? I think I need to rethink the consequences ...' The door clicked shut, muffling Mrs Beanscough's voice.

Unable to hear any more, Grace hurried back along the corridor, grateful that the history block (her first subject of the day) was close to the office. When she arrived at her classroom, she took a deep breath and pushed the door open.

The room fell silent.

Everyone looked up.

'Page 49, Grace. Economic upheaval in 19th Century Britain and the rise of the Luddite movement.' Her teacher, Mr Jensen, turned back to the whiteboard and continued to talk to the class as he wrote. 'Popular opinion, even now, is that the Luddites were against all advancements in technology, however ...' Grace's burning ears blocked out the teacher as she searched for a desk, aware that all eyes were still on her. Finally, she spotted an empty chair and gratefully flung herself onto it before reaching into her backpack and pulling out her history textbook, notepad and pencil case. She gently placed the carrier bag containing her new coat inside the main compartment, stowed it under her chair and turned to page 49.

'Check Grace out!' a voice sniggered from directly behind. Then, in a stage whisper, 'Did you get dressed in the dark today, Grace?'

Grace inwardly groaned. In her haste to sit down, she hadn't noticed there was a reason the seat was vacant. It was right in front of Jill Blackburn and her gang. And she was still wearing her old coat.

Grace quickly yanked off her coat and sank lower in her chair, her cheeks flaming. She fixed her eyes on the page in front of her, acutely aware of the glances and giggles of her classmates. To her horror, she noticed the new boy, Abeer Prashad, was looking over too.

'And you think *that's* an improvement?' Jill snorted.

'Is there something you'd like to share with the class, Miss Blackburn?' Mr Jensen enquired as he continued to write on the board.

'No, sir, just discussing the socioeconomic conditions that led to the Luddite uprising,' she replied sweetly. 'It really is fascinating.'

'Yes. Quite. I'll look forward to seeing your work at the end of class, Miss Blackburn,' Mr Jensen replied. Grace smiled to herself as the sound of frantically turned pages came from behind, followed by the scratch of biro on paper.

Thankfully, the rest of the lesson passed uneventfully, and when the bell rang, Grace raced out while Jill Blackburn was stuck talking to Mr Jensen. The tension drained from her the moment she stepped out of the classroom, knowing that Jill wouldn't be with her in the next class, DT. The design and technology suite was situated in an annexe across the main playground, and Grace joined the steady stream of pupils heading outside. There was a bin just by the entrance to the classroom, and she thrust her old coat inside before pushing through the doors.

Learning from her mistake in history, Grace found a seat at the very back of the classroom and placed her bag on the empty seat next to her. DT was her least favourite lesson, so she usually did the bare minimum required to get through it. But today, their brief was to design a logo for the side of a festival food truck. She quickly pulled her sketching pencils from her backpack and began to doodle. Her pencil glided across the page as she formed the letters of the company name in graffiti. Grace's Grub. Then she pulled out her colours and began smudging and highlighting, outlining and shading, making the letters come alive on the page. She was utterly engrossed until the harsh trill of the school bell tugged her back to reality. She glanced at the clock on the wall behind her. She'd been drawing for almost an hour, but it'd only felt like five minutes.

'Excellent, Grace. What a wonderful sign!' Miss Chen exclaimed, glancing over Grace's shoulder. 'You really have a talent for street art.'

'Thanks, Miss,' Grace replied with a smile as she packed her bag and stood to leave the classroom.

Even the prospect of detention couldn't dampen her spirits, and she was still smiling when she entered the *Consequence Classroom*. Suzy was already there, staring glumly at the towering piles of leaflets on the desk in front of her. Grace picked up a brown paper bag off the chair next to Suzy and sat down before peering inside.

'You don't want to know,' Suzy muttered.

She really didn't. Inside was an unwrapped sandwich, the ham turning brown and curling at the edges. The bread was scaly to the touch.

'Urgh!' she cried, pushing it away. 'Is yours the same?'

'Yep. Every single time. They could at least wrap them, but I guess that's part of the punishment,' Suzy said. At that moment, Mrs Beanscough strode into the room and stopped directly in front of them.

'On your desks, there are 1,500 leaflets advertising the end of term ball. They need to be folded in half and put into piles ready to be distributed. The number required for each class is indicated on this form.' She placed a piece of paper on the desk next to the piles. 'They must all be folded by the end of lunch, or I will see you tomorrow lunchtime, and the one after if needs be, until the task is complete.' She paused, looking at the girls and then pointedly at her watch. 'What are you waiting for?' she asked before turning and striding back out of the room.

'This will take forever!' Grace moaned.

'Don't worry, I'll be able to get some done after school if we don't finish now.' Suzy picked up the first leaflet.

'You mean …?'

'Yep. Double detention. That cow Beany's got it in for me, I swear.' She angrily pressed the fold, not caring whether it was straight, and slammed it next to the unfolded leaflets.

It was going to be a long, long lunch hour.

CHAPTER 3

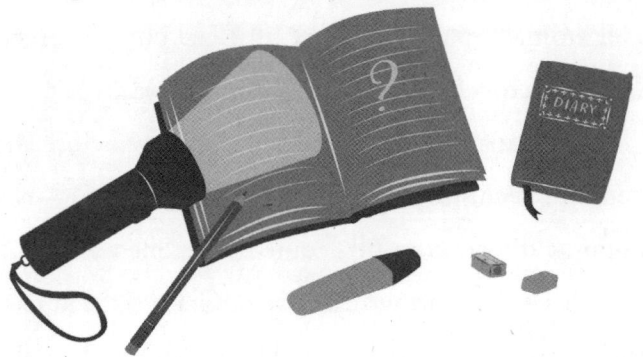

After an hour of folding leaflets, the afternoon's French and geography classes seemed to pass quickly, and in no time, the end of day bell rang. Grace grabbed her bag and found herself being swept down the corridor and out of the school's double doors in a noisy wave of teens, all eager to put as much distance between themselves and the school as possible.

All around her, kids loosened ties and chatted about their plans for the evening before breaking off into smaller groups to make their way home. Grace scanned the sea of faces to see if anyone she knew was heading her way, but there was only one person she recognised. Her stomach plummeted as Jill Blackburn emerged from the crowds and headed straight towards her.

Grace turned and hurried out of view before she could be seen, turning left onto the high street – the opposite direction to Jill's route home. She was safe.

With a new spring in her step, Grace strolled past the shops, waving to her neighbour, Mrs Peel, as she walked across the road from her shop.

'Hi Grace! Did you manage to get a coat? Suzy told me about your emergency this morning when she dropped off my tea,' Mrs Peel called.

'I did – and it's the nicest coat you've ever seen!' Grace grinned.

'Well, if it's as chilly tomorrow morning as it was this morning, you'll have to drop by and show me. I do love a good charity shop find!' Mrs Peel paused. 'Oh, hello Jill, love. Don't often see you this way after school. Has your mum got you doing errands?'

Grace spun around – it couldn't be! But it was. There, a few steps behind, was Jill Blackburn and her best friend Debbie Gribbs. They must be going to Debbie's house the next road along from Grace's, and if they were, they'd be following her the whole way home.

Eager to avoid them, Grace slipped into an alley on her left that would take her around the back of the shops and out of Jill Blackburn's way. She regretted it immediately, her eyes watering as the stench of rotting rubbish hit her.

The narrow passageway was lined with piles of bin bags, many of them split and spewing their putrid contents onto the floor. Knowing she couldn't go back to the high street, Grace covered her nose and mouth with the crook of her elbow and hurried onwards. After a few steps, the alley split left and right so that it ran parallel to the main road. Grace quickly stepped to the right, stopped and listened.

Had she been spotted?

She strained her ears to find out.

'See ya, Mrs Peel.'

'Bye, Jill. Remind your mum to bring back that vase I lent her, won't you?'

'Yeah, will do!'

'But you broke the vase last week,' came Debbie's whispered reply.

'Yeah, but she doesn't know that, does she?!' The sniggers of the two girls disappeared into the distance.

Grace glanced down the length of the alley – the bin bags were mainly at the entrance, ready to be collected by the rubbish truck. The rest of the passage was clear and wouldn't smell for much longer, so she decided to stick to the alleyway rather than risk another close encounter.

It was much colder in the shadows of the alley than out on the main road, and Grace shivered, rubbing her bare arms for warmth. Quickly, she pulled the backpack off her shoulders and took out her new coat. Then she slipped her arms inside the silken sleeves and shrugged it onto her shoulders. It felt as familiar as if she'd owned it all of her life. Smiling to herself, Grace bent to pick up her backpack. As she did, a sudden wave of dizziness washed over her, and she reached a hand out to the wall for support.

Her heart raced and blackness flooded the edges of her vision. *What was happening?* Grace crouched down and dropped her head between her knees, just as she'd been taught in first aid class at school. She concentrated on slowing her breathing.

In, out.

In … out.

In …

… out.

Gradually, her pulse slowed, and the edges of her vision began to clear. Misty patches of colour formed and slowly sharpened until she could see clearly again.

But she wasn't in the alley any more.

She was at the entrance to a huge living room. A square of four long, white leather sofas took up most of the room. An oval glass table, strewn with magazines, sat in the centre of them. Beyond the sofas was an enormous window which looked out over a vast lawned garden. Heavy golden curtains were elegantly draped on either side and tied in place with plaited rope.

Then, the scene moved from left to right even though Grace was certain she wasn't moving her head. It was as if she was looking through someone else's eyes. Someone who was clearly looking for something. Finally, they fixed their gaze on a black leather clip-top bag that had been left at one corner of the sofa. They moved towards it, picked it up and twisted the clasp. Their eyes darted towards the door then back to the bag before pulling out a handful of strange-looking money.

'Olivia? What are *you doing?!'*

Smudges of darkness slipped across her vision before fading once more. Grace was almost surprised to find herself back in the alley. She shook her head and blinked. What *had* happened? Had she fallen and bumped her head? She reached up a shaking hand and tentatively tested her scalp. Nothing. Had she fainted? It had never happened before, but what other explanation was there? But then, it had all seemed so … real! With shaking legs, Grace rose to her feet and stumbled out of the alley and back into the sunshine of the high street.

'Oi! Watch where you're going!' a cyclist shouted as he swerved around her on the pavement.

Grace leapt back, her heart thundering in her chest. She had to get home. Quickly. Keeping her head down, she weaved through the pedestrians milling around on the pavement until, finally, her house came into view. She jogged through the wrought iron gate and up the three steps that led to her front door and fumbled the key into the lock.

'Grace? Is that you?' Her mum was *still* in the office.

'Yeah, Mum. I'm just going to my room!' she called back and hurried up the stairs to the sanctuary of her bedroom. Still shaking, she stood in front of the mirror. She looked perfectly normal. A little paler perhaps, but still herself. She ran a trembling hand through her hair and perched on the edge of the bed.

What *had* happened?

Then it hit her.

Lunch! She hadn't touched the sandwich in detention, so she hadn't eaten a thing all day. Stupid,

stupid, stupid! No wonder she'd passed out. She shook her head at her own foolishness and carefully took off her coat. Reaching into the wardrobe, she pushed the existing hangers to one side to make room and hung it in the new space. After a quick stroke of the sleeve, she closed the door and hurried back downstairs to the kitchen.

It was her favourite room in the house. No matter what the weather was like outside, the glow of the honey-coloured oak cupboards made the room seem like a sunny oasis. Grace instantly felt like herself again. She opened the fridge door in search of a snack and pulled out a bowl of pasta left over from last night's dinner.

Perfect.

Putting her strange episode behind her, she grabbed a fork, pulled out a stool from the breakfast bar and sat to eat.

CHAPTER 4

The next day, Suzy called for Grace as usual.

'Ready?'

'Yep!' Grace grabbed her school bag from the hall table, pulled on her coat and closed the door behind her.

'How did the detention go?' Grace asked. 'Did you manage to get all the leaflets done?'

'Yeah,' Suzy sighed. 'I never want to see another leaflet ever again! I swear Beany sneaked some extras on the pile while we were in class. There were *loads*!'

'At least your hands will get a rest this morning.' Grace laughed.

'Hmmm. Not sure which'd be worse though – folding more leaflets or watching this stupid film in a crummy old cinema,' Suzy moaned.

'Oh, it might be alright. I've never seen a really old film before, and Miss Wilcock said it'll be a more authentic experience if we watch it in an old cinema. I'm quite looking forward to it actually!'

Suzy harrumphed, unconvinced. 'The only thing I'm looking forward to is not having to go back to school afterwards. Miss Wilcock rocks for arranging this on a Friday when we finish at lunch anyway!'

They walked on until they reached the small arthouse cinema at the end of the high street. Outside, posters advertised films they'd never heard of – *Charly*, *Maya*, *In Fabric* – none of the usual blockbusters. Their drama teacher, Miss Wilcock, greeted them at the entrance.

'Morning, girls. Here are your tickets and a workbook to complete afterwards.' She smiled, handing them the items. 'The owner said we have the cinema to ourselves this morning, so you can sit wherever you like.'

Grace thanked her, returning the smile, while Suzy just grunted and walked through the doorway.

Inside was like no cinema Grace had ever been to. The room was tiny, almost like a large living room. One side was taken up by a floor-to-ceiling, red velvet curtain. In front of this were five rows of crimson velvet flip-down seats, each with a small brass plaque displaying a seat number. Over half were already occupied by their classmates, and the room was abuzz with chatter.

Grace squinted in the dim light to find a seat. 'Come on, there's a good spot over there,' she said, leading Suzy to two free seats right in the middle of the room. Discarded popcorn crunched underfoot, and their feet stuck slightly to the tacky carpet as they sidled along the row of seats.

'These look great,' Suzy said, pulling down a seat and flopping into it. She squinted at her ticket in the darkness. 'What're we watching again?'

'*Charly*. I've never heard of it, but it *could* be alright,' Grace replied as she took off her coat. She lowered herself into the seat next to her friend, then settled back with her coat across her lap, to watch the other students arrive.

One by one, the rest of the seats were filled. Just as the last person sat down, the lights dimmed and an excited murmur rippled through the auditorium. The huge curtain slowly slid open, and the screen behind flickered to life.

Grace couldn't tear her eyes away. How had she never watched an old film before? Even Suzy had stopped her grumbling about how rubbish it was going to be. The film was set in the 1960s, and Grace was fascinated by the clothes and cars and technology. It was all so different! As she watched, the main character entered a hotel and Grace blinked in surprise. The decor was really similar to the house in her vision. The crystal chandeliers, the gold, the curved lines of the furniture. It wasn't the *same*, but it was clearly the same period.

She continued to watch, slightly distracted now,

a thousand thoughts darting around her head. *How had she imagined a house from the 1960s if she'd never seen one before today?* She sat forwards in her seat and drank in every detail. On screen, the main character was in a sitting room, and the camera slowly panned across to a lady who was standing next to a fireplace. A huge ornate mirror hung above it, and as the camera moved across its reflective surface, darkness pressed in from the edges of Grace's vision, just as it had in the alley the day before.

She was looking in a full-length mirror. Only, the face that looked back wasn't hers. It was a girl about her age with a sleek golden bob set into perfect curls around her face. She wore a short, blue, sleeveless dress which was fitted to the waist and then flared out to just above the knee. Her skin was the palest ivory, and as Grace looked on, she pinched her cheeks, then turned her face this way and that to check the colour. Next, she opened a small, light pink lipstick and dabbed it onto her lips before pressing them together.

'Bye – I'm going now!' she called before grabbing a

dark green velvet coat and skipping out of the front door.

It was a beautiful day.

The sun made the white gravel on the great curving driveway sparkle like diamonds, and butterflies fluttered around the flowerbeds as she made her way to the side of the house. Just around the corner, up against the wall, was a pastel blue bike with a wicker basket perched at the front. The girl folded her coat and placed it in the basket then pulled the bike clear, turned it around and mounted it before pedalling down the drive. She dinged the little silver bell on the handlebars and waved behind her as the house disappeared into the distance.

Grace's vision cleared and she lurched to her feet. 'I've got to get out of here,' she whispered to Suzy before edging along the seats, muttering her apologies as she bumped past knees and toes. Suzy leapt up and followed, picking up Grace's coat from the floor.

'Is everything okay?' Miss Wilcock asked as they passed her seat by the exit.

'Yeah, just going to the toilet. Back in a minute.' Miss Wilcock nodded and Suzy hurried through the door and joined Grace.

'What is it? You look terrible,' Suzy asked, noticing how pale Grace looked.

'I ... I'm not sure. One minute I was watching the film, and the next I was seeing out of the eyes of a young girl who was looking in a mirror and getting ready to go out.'

'So, you fell asleep and had a dream about a girl?' Suzy suggested.

Grace shook her head but didn't answer. Whatever she said would sound crazy.

'What is it? There's something you're not telling me, isn't there?' Suzy demanded.

Grace blew out her cheeks. 'It wasn't a dream. I know it wasn't because it happened yesterday too.'

'When?'

'When I was walking home from school. I didn't say anything because I thought I'd just fainted from not eating lunch. But now I know it's not that,' she admitted.

Suzy was quiet as she took in what her friend

had said.

'There's something else too,' she paused, barely believing what she was about to say. 'I … I think the coat is giving me visions.'

'What? How—'

'I saw it, Suze. The coat. The girl grabbed a dark green velvet coat. It looked exactly the same as *that* coat,' she said, gesturing towards the coat in Suzy's arms. '*And* she had a blue bike with a wicker basket on the front just like the one the old lady wheeled out of the charity shop before I went in!'

'But that doesn't mean it wasn't a dream,' Suzy said. 'People dream about random stuff all the time.'

'Yeah, but I *know* I didn't fall asleep just now *or* in the alley yesterday. I'm telling you, it's the coat!'

Suzy held her hands up. 'Okay, okay! How about we test it then?' she suggested. 'You put the coat back on, and I'll watch to see what happens. We could go to your house and do it after the film's finished,' Suzy added. 'After all, we've got the whole afternoon free.'

'Actually Suze, I don't think I'm up for it today.'

'Okay, shall we do it tomorrow then? I'll come over to yours after breakfast,' Suzy said. 'But right now, we'd better go back in before Miss Wilcock comes looking for us.' Grace nodded, forcing a smile, and followed Suzy back into the auditorium. But deep down, she wasn't so sure she wanted to test it out. If it was the coat causing the visions, then she'd know there was nothing wrong with her. But if it wasn't, seeing things that weren't there could never be a good sign.

When Grace got home after the film, she headed straight for the kitchen and put the kettle on before spooning three heaped teaspoons of chocolate powder into a mug. As she waited for the kettle to boil, she took off her coat, tossing it onto a stool as she crossed to the biscuit cupboard. With a whisper, the coat's silken lining slipped off the stool's leather surface and it tumbled to the floor. Grace grabbed a pack of custard creams then picked the coat up, but as she did, her fingers brushed against a small bulge in the bottom of the coat's lining. Frowning, she placed the biscuits on the counter and took a closer look, her fingers probing the length of the hem. There it was again. There was definitely something stuck inside the lining.

She turned the coat inside out, searching for a hole in the seams where an object might have slipped inside, but the stitching was intact. Next, she checked the pockets, turning them inside out to get a better look. There it was. A badly mended hole.

Grace grabbed a pair of manicure scissors from the first aid kit and gently snipped the threads, revealing a small opening. She turned the coat upside down and carefully guided the object towards the hole. In no time, the corner of a small dark red object poked through, and Grace eased it out. Her heart skipped a beat as the wording on the cover was revealed.

Diary.

Ever so carefully, she opened the first page.

OM
1969

PRIVATE!!!

Grace could hardly breathe as she turned the next page. It was the diary of the person who had owned the coat!

This page was filled with a series of numbers and letters, all written in meticulously neat handwriting.

12.1 12:15 HP
15.1 H final KM
16.1 17:00 UH
18.1 JB?

She flicked through page after page, but they were all the same. Sighing, she placed the book on the kitchen counter and finished making her hot chocolate, her mind whirring, trying to decipher the text.

By the time she'd finished her drink, Grace was still no nearer to working out the mysterious diary entries, but she did know a coding expert. Suzy. And she would be round in the morning.

CHAPTER 5

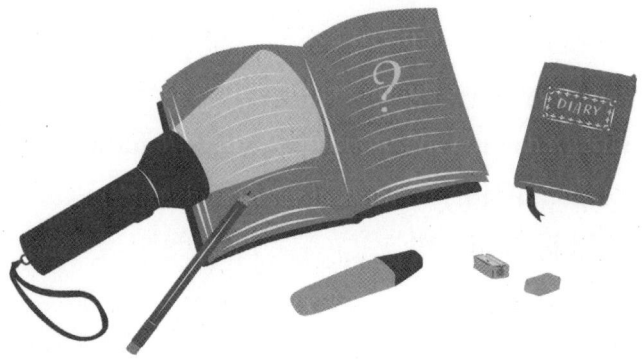

Grace woke to bright sunshine streaming through the curtains, yet a heavy cloud hung over her. Suzy would be coming over soon, and she still didn't know what to think about their 'test'. If she wore the coat again, she knew she'd be inviting a vision, and the feeling of someone else's consciousness seeping into her mind, and the disorientation she felt afterwards, was horrible. But if they didn't test it, she'd never know for sure if it was the coat causing them or something else.

She gave herself a mental shake and flung off the covers. Well, whatever it was, she'd know soon enough. Grace pulled on the skinny jeans she'd discarded on the floor next to the bed last night and rifled through her wardrobe for a jumper. While she was sliding the hangers over, her hand brushed against the coat. She took it out and lay it on her bed ready for later. Returning to the wardrobe, she tugged a cream jumper off its hanger and pulled it on before running downstairs.

'Morning, Mum!' she called as she passed the office on her way to the kitchen.

'Morning, love. There's bread in the toaster and fresh orange juice on the counter if you want it.'

Grace stepped into the kitchen and winced as the chill from the floor tiles seeped into her toes. She gingerly tiptoed across to the toaster, pushed the bread down and then scurried out to grab a pair of slippers from the hallway. Feet now snug, she returned to the kitchen and gulped down the glass of juice her mum had left before pouring a second one. She returned the juice carton to the fridge and grabbed some butter just as the toast popped up.

Awesome timing, she congratulated herself. Maybe today *was* going to be a good day after all?

She smoothed the butter on the toast and put the tub back in the fridge, glancing at the clock as she settled back at the breakfast bar. It was five minutes until Suzy was due to arrive.

The minute hand seemed to creep around the clock face, but before she had finished her second slice of toast, the doorbell chimed.

Ding-dong! Tap! Tap! Tap!

Grace held the last half of her toast between her teeth and put her plate and glass in the dishwasher before rushing to the door.

'Morning!' Suzy grinned as she stepped past Grace and into the hallway. 'And what a beautiful morning it is!'

Grace feigned concern. 'Are you feeling okay?' She placed the back of her hand against Suzy's forehead. 'Hmmm, you could be coming down with something …' Suzy batted her hand away, laughing.

'Ha, ha! Am I not allowed to be happy first thing in the morning? Good morning, Mrs Yi,' she called out.

'Morning, Suzy. Help yourself to breakfast,' Grace's mum called back.

Suzy turned to Grace. 'I was so excited this morning I got up hours ago, so I'm already breakfasted and two cups of coffee in.'

'That explains a lot!' Grace quipped with a grin.

'Are you ready to be a guinea pig? I can't wait to see what happens when you put the coat on!'

'Shh! Keep your voice down!' Grace hissed, gesturing towards the office door.

'Sorry!' Suzy grinned, not looking in the slightest bit sorry. 'Let's go to your room and get started.'

She ran up the stairs, leaving Grace following reluctantly behind. As Grace entered her room, Suzy was fixing a small tripod to her phone.

'I thought we could video everything. So, if something did happen, we could watch it back afterwards. What d'you think?'

Grace wasn't sure she'd want to watch it back if

anything *did* happen, but she nodded anyway. After all, what were the chances that she'd have a blackout today?

Suzy placed the phone on the dressing table and peered around at the screen. She adjusted it a little then straightened up.

'That should do it – it'll record most of that side of the room and the bed so we'll catch it all as long as you stay over there.' She held out both arms to indicate the space. 'Give me the thumbs up when you're ready to put the coat on.'

Grace stepped over to the bed and gave Suzy a shaky smile. *Why am I so nervous if nothing is going to happen?*

She raised her thumb and picked up the coat.

The phone beeped as Suzy pressed record, and she perched on the dressing table to watch.

Grace slowly pulled the coat on and fastened the buttons.

Nothing happened.

'That's it, then. It's not the coat,' she said, starting to undo the buttons.

'Hang on a minute! Give it a chance!' Her friend picked up the phone and walked towards her, videoing all the while. 'Maybe we need to go outside or watch an old film or something?' she suggested.

Grace gave an exasperated sigh, lowering her hands from the buttons. 'Nothing. Is going. To happen.'

'Well, in that case, it can't harm to try for a bit longer, can it?' Suzy persisted, stepping backwards through the bedroom door, her phone still pointing at Grace.

Grace shook her head, muttering under her breath, but followed Suzy out of the room.

'You'll need to walk slowly, so I don't fall down the stairs,' Suzy said, one hand on the phone, the other on the banister as she continued to walk backwards.

Grace followed her friend to the bottom of the stairs. 'Now what?' she asked.

'I reckon the garden. That way, if anything happens, you're somewhere safe and no one will see.' Grace started to walk towards the kitchen, but Suzy held out a hand to stop her. 'Let me go in front. I want to be able to catch your face if something does happen.' She squeezed past Grace in the narrow hallway and again stepped backwards, Grace following behind.

When they got to the back door that led out into the garden, Suzy reached behind her and twisted the key in the lock before pushing the door and stepping outside. She stopped suddenly.

'Urgh! The sun's playing havoc with the video. Just stay there while I change the settings.' She swiped and pressed at the screen for a few seconds then gestured for Grace to follow.

This is ridiculous, Grace thought. She was already uncomfortably warm from wearing the coat inside the house, and a small bead of sweat trickled down her side.

'Come on, Suzy! I'm baking. If I *do* have a weird turn, it'll be from heatstroke not the coat!' She reached up again to undo the buttons, but her fingers never got there. The now-familiar sensation of drifting filled her mind, and her vision grew dark.

She was looking out across open grassland. A boy stood next to her, but she couldn't see his face. 'I can't stay long,' came the girl's voice. 'I told Mother I was going to Georgie's house, so she'll be expecting me soon.'

'Oh, come on, Liv, ten minutes won't harm. I'll take your photo. If I take a good one you can use it to impress those modelling scouts you keep talking about,' he said, raising the Polaroid camera that hung from a leather strap around his neck.

'You know I want to stay,' Liv replied, taking a step back. 'But it's difficult.'

'It's always difficult,' the boy spat before drinking from a bottle of cola clutched in his right hand. 'I don't know why I bother. You know, I could have any girl my own age. Any girl I want. It'd be less hassle than going out with you.'

'But Johnny …'

'What, Liv? I bet you didn't even manage to get the money, did you? Even though you know I'm broke after my allowance got stopped. The least you can do is stay and spend some time with me.' Johnny stepped towards her, but Liv took another step backwards.

'Next time, Johnny. I promise.' Liv glanced at her watch. 'I've really got to go now …'

Grace's vision dimmed then cleared. She looked over at Suzy who was staring at her, open-mouthed. Her friend rushed over.

'Are you okay?' Suzy asked, her forehead creased with concern.

'Yes … I think so,' Grace replied, taking off the coat and swiping at the sweat that was trickling into her eyes. She sat down heavily on the grass and told Suzy what she'd seen.

'Okay, so it's definitely the coat. Agreed?' Suzy asked when they were back in Grace's bedroom.

'As crazy as it sounds, yeah. I think you could be right.' Grace's eyes fell on the phone. 'Let's have a look at the video.'

Suzy looked surprised to see the phone still in her hands. 'Hang on a sec.' She fiddled with the screen before walking around the bed to sit next to Grace. 'Here.' She held the phone out between them and tapped *Play* with her thumb.

The image of Grace putting on the coat appeared on the screen. 'Skip to the bit in the garden, Suze.' Her friend swiped her finger across the screen until it showed Grace stepping through the kitchen door, blurred as it fought against the brightness of the sun, and then came back into focus.

It was strange seeing herself on the screen. She was surprised how grumpy and uncomfortable she looked. Her hair was already dampening along her scalp. 'Come on, Suzy! It's too hot for this …' she was saying and reaching up to undo the buttons. On the screen, her face went slack, and her eyes rolled upwards.

'There – look there – that's when it happened!' she cried.

Suzy's voice could be heard in the background, 'Grace? Grace? Are you alright?' then the picture tumbled down and just showed grass as Suzy dropped the phone. Her friend's feet came into the shot as she crouched next to Grace, then the lens was completely blocked by a dark mass.

'Blast! I missed most of it.' Suzy poked angrily at the screen, stopping and starting the footage. 'That's it.' She ran her fingers through her short pink hair. 'The rest is just grass and my bum blocking out everything else. I can't see you at all.' She flung the phone down on the bed. 'One thing's certain, though – you'll have to return the coat.'

Grace had remained silent through this, but now turned to her friend and sighed. 'I don't know, Suze. What if I'm *meant* to have the coat? What if it's trying to tell me something?' She held her hand up as Suzy opened her mouth to speak. 'Just hear me out. All three visions have been of the same girl – I'm sure of that – and it feels like they're kind of telling a story – like I *have* to keep watching to find out what happens.' She looked at Suzy, who was quiet for a moment. 'Plus, I found this.' She picked up the tiny diary and held it out to Suzy. 'It'd fallen into the lining through a hole in one of the pockets.'

Suzy flicked through the pages.

'But what does it say? It's just a jumble of numbers

and letters.'

'I know. I was kind of hoping you'd be able to help with that. It must all mean *something*; we just need to work out what.'

'Okay.' Suzy snapped photos of the first few pages with her phone. 'I'll take a look at these and see what I can work out. But listen. You can't wear the coat again until we figure out what's going on. What if you have a vision when you're walking across a road? Or walking downstairs? You could get hurt!'

'You're right. How about if I only wear it when I'm with you ... and you can keep videoing me if you like so we can see it after?'

'Okay,' Suzy conceded. 'But never, ever, wear it without me – deal?'

'Deal.' Grace smiled at Suzy. 'So ... how about we try it again now?'

Suzy shook her head but returned her smile. 'For someone who was reluctant to test the coat, you're very persistent!' She picked up her phone and pressed record.

Grace pulled on the coat once again and waited.

Nothing.

'Let's go outside again,' she suggested, and they hurried back out to the garden. She sat in a small patch of shade under an apple tree at the end of the garden and waited.

'Anything?' Suzy asked.

Grace shook her head.

Five minutes passed.

Ten minutes.

Fifteen.

Grace's shoulders slumped.

'We'll try again tomorrow,' Suzy said, reaching out a hand to pull Grace to her feet. 'I'm sure you'll see something then. You know what though? I was thinking about everything last night, and I think you might be psychic.'

'What?'

'Psychic. You know, can see things that other people can't.'

'I know what it means, Suze, but no way am I psychic!' Grace laughed.

'Think about it. Last year you knew where to find Scruff when he'd escaped again. *No one* knew where to even start looking, but the minute you picked up his lead you seemed to know exactly where he'd be. Then there was our Year 6 residential. Remember the epic game of hide and seek where Paul Santini hid up a tree and no one could find him, so we decided to go in for tea, figuring he'd follow?' Grace nodded. 'You picked up his hoodie to take it in with us in case he forgot it, and all of a sudden, you knew where he was hiding. How d'you explain that?'

'They were just a coincidence. Two things in a lifetime does not make me psychic.'

'You say that now, but they're just two times I could think of off the top of my head. I reckon, if I put my mind to it, I could come up with other things. Anyway, just think about it,' Suzy persisted. 'Now though, I'd better be getting home. I told Mum I'd only be an hour and I've been more than that already. She wants me to go shopping for an outfit for my cousin's wedding next weekend.' She pulled a face.

Grace couldn't help but smile. She knew how much her friend hated clothes shopping, and an afternoon being dragged into clothes shop after clothes shop was her idea of hell. 'I'll think of you when I'm sat here watching TV,' she joked.

'Some friend you are!' Suzy punched her lightly on the arm. 'If I'm not in school on Monday, tell them it was death by shopping!' She waved over her shoulder as she opened the front door and walked down the path towards her home on the street behind Grace's.

Grace laughed to herself and closed the door. Then, she walked back to her bedroom, pulling off her coat as she went. The coat hanger was still on her bed from earlier and she picked it up and slid her coat onto it. As she reached towards the wardrobe to hang it up, shadows tugged at the edge of her vision. She gripped the wardrobe door just as everything went dark.

'If you leave now, then that's it. We're done.'

'Then it's over, Johnny,' Liv sobbed, turning to walk away. 'I've got to get to Joan's before Mother finds out I'm not there.'

'Don't you walk away from me!' Johnny lunged forwards and grabbed Liv's wrist, swinging her round to face him.

'Let go! You're hurting me!' Liv cried. She tried to yank her arm free, but his grip was too strong.

'You think you can end it just like that?' Johnny snarled. *'We're over when I say we're over. Understand?'*

'I said get off me!' Liv shouted, pushing him as hard as she could with her free hand. Johnny took a step back, but as he did, his foot struck against a large rock causing him to stumble. He released Liv's wrist, his arms pinwheeling to regain his balance but she could tell it was futile. And when he hit the floor, he would be furious. Liv didn't hesitate. She started to sprint to her bike, but she'd barely taken a step when the sound of shattering glass and a cry of pain stopped her in her tracks. She quickly glanced back at Johnny. He was kneeling on the floor cradling his left hand. The bottom of the cola bottle was embedded in his palm and blood poured from the wound. Liv hurried back and crouched next to him just as he'd pulled the glass free.

'Johnny, I'm sorry. I didn't mean to hurt you. Are you alr–'

'Alright?' he said in a voice that was dangerously calm. He staggered to his feet, looming above her, the broken bottle clutched in his good hand. 'Yeah. I'm just great,' he added with a mirthless laugh. 'But I'm not sure the same can be said about you.' He raised the broken bottle and thrust it downwards in a deadly arc.

Grace gasped as she came out of her trance, her entire body trembling.

That was it. That was *why* the coat was giving her visions. Liv had it with her when she was murdered.

CHAPTER 6

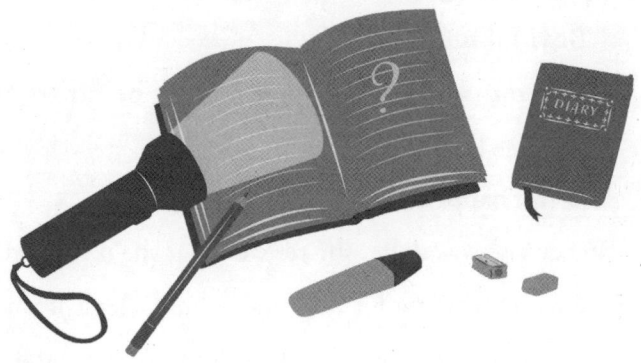

She raced to her bedside table, yanked open the top drawer and fumbled around inside. In no time, she'd found what she was looking for. She grabbed the notepad and sketched an image of what she had seen, every now and then closing her eyes to conjure a more vivid picture before scribbling down any extra details. When she was happy with what she'd drawn, she turned the page and wrote down as much as she could remember about the visions:

* **Girl: Liv (Olivia) – rich – big house, chandelier, grand piano in sitting room, gold curtains, high ceilings.**
* **Boy: Johnny – older?**
* **Met on open grassland. Couldn't be far from home – Liv cycled there.**
* **What happened to the bike?**

When she was done, she reread what she'd written. There really wasn't a lot to go on – but at least it was something. What to do with the information, though? Grace went to the kitchen and made a hot chocolate, studying her notes as she drank. Questions crowded her mind, but one single thought pushed to the front. *Is Liv real?* She wrote it in her notebook, underlining it several times. This was what she needed to find out. She needed to know if Liv really existed or whether she was a figment of her imagination. But how?

Grace finished off her hot chocolate and was just putting her cup in the dishwasher when a thought struck her. When they'd had to research the building of the local canal, they'd visited the library to look at different sources of information, from books, to microfiche, to the census. The library would hold local newspapers, and if Liv *was* real and *had* gone missing, then there would be a newspaper report about it.

She dashed back to her bedroom and grabbed her purse. She opened it and rummaged through its contents. Not finding what she was looking for, she walked around the bed and pulled open the top drawer of her bedside table. There, on top of a pile of loyalty reward cards, was her library card. She snatched it up, added it to her purse and hurried out of her room.

'I'm going to the library! I'll sort my own lunch out!' she shouted to her mum, not waiting for a reply before rushing out of the house.

Grace studied the bus timetable, trailing her finger down the list of destinations. Chesterford Town Centre. 10:15. Two minutes.

She pulled out her phone and texted Suzy:

GONE 2 LIBRARY. HAD ANOTHER VISION. LIV DEAD!!! GOING 2 C WHAT CAN FIND OUT. COME

WHEN YOU'RE DONE WITH YOUR MUM.

She pressed send then smiled and began typing again.

IF YOU'RE STILL ALIVE (😉).

Grace put her phone back in her bag just as a bus rounded the corner. The sign above the windscreen read 12A. It was her bus. She stuck out her arm to flag it down, and it slowed to a stop just in front of her.

The doors slid open, and Grace climbed the steep steps onto the bus. 'The town centre, please,' she said.

'£1.40,' the driver grunted, without looking at her. Grace held her phone up to the payment point and waited for a tick to appear on her screen before making her way to the back of the bus. She sat down and shuffled across to the window seat, but she didn't see a single thing she passed. Her head was filled with questions about the mysterious girl called Liv.

Before she knew it, the bus had reached her stop and she found herself in front of the library. She pushed open the heavy glass door and was instantly greeted by the smell of books. Grace felt herself relax as she walked among the bookcases to the help desk in the middle of the room.

The lady behind the desk was scanning returned books and placing them on a trolley, but immediately looked up as Grace approached.

'Can I help you?' she asked, smiling.

'Hi, um ... do you keep copies of old newspapers here, please?'

'Yes, which one do you need?'

'I, er, don't really know.' She thought for a moment. 'It'd be from the 1960s.'

'That's a long period of time. Can you narrow it down at all?' the librarian asked.

'Um ... there might be something that could help,' Grace replied, pulling out her phone. She typed in *Charly* film. It was released in 1968. If the decor in the film was similar to the house in her vision, maybe they were from roughly the same time. 'Okay, how about 1965 to maybe 1970? Would that help?'

'That's still a long time, but it's not a problem. Is it a local or national newspaper you need?'

'Local, I think.'

'Right, then I'd start with *The Cheshire Observer* – it was only printed once a week rather than every day, so that'll save you having to read through a daily paper if you're not sure of a specific date. I'll set you up on computer C upstairs. Here are the login details you'll need. Give me five minutes and I'll have it all up and running for you.'

Grace took the slip of paper with her username and password written on it, thanked the lady and made her way to the staircase at the rear of the library. As she walked along the central aisle, a high-pitched squeal of delight caught her attention.

'Alright, alright, let me turn the page then!' a familiar voice replied. Grace peered around the bookcase to her right. Abeer was kneeling on the rug in the centre of the picture book section with a toddler sat astride his back like a mini rodeo rider. A book was propped open in front of him, and he reached out to turn the page.

The girl leant forwards excitedly, clearly knowing what came next.

'I'm a big, scary bear!' Abeer growled, pulling an angry bear face and stomping his 'feet'. 'And big, scary bears aren't for riding! What you want is a horse!'

The girl giggled and replied, 'How will I know it's a horse?'

'Simple. Horses trot like this,' he said. The girl sat forwards on Abeer's back and gripped his t-shirt tightly as he rose up onto his hands and feet and proceeded to 'trot' around the rug. Too late, he spotted Grace and froze mid-trot, a look of embarrassed horror on his face.

'Um, hi,' he said, not quite meeting her eyes.

'Hello!' The little girl waved at Grace.

'Grace, meet Anya, my little sister.'

'Hi Anya. That looks like a fine horse you've got there.' Grace smiled.

'It's not a horse, silly. It's a bear!' Anya giggled, then turned back to Abeer. 'Next page!' she demanded.

'I'll leave you to it! See you in school,' Grace said and continued upstairs, giggles and cries of 'giddy up!'

coming from behind her.

When she reached the computer stations on the first floor, there was only one other person there – an elderly gentleman whose workstation was covered with sticky notes and drawings of what looked to Grace like a family tree. He looked up when he heard her approach, acknowledged her with a brief nod and then returned to his computer.

Grace's station was on the next bank of desks, so she had the whole section to herself. She pulled out the wheeled chair and sat down before taking the notepad and pen out of her bag. Quickly, she reread her notes and checked her watch.

Two minutes to go.

She tapped her fingers on the keyboard, impatient to get going. From the other bank of computers, the old man cleared his throat loudly and frowned at Grace. She smiled an apology and whipped her hand away from the keys. Needing to be doing *something*, she pulled the slip of paper that the librarian had given her out of her pocket and spread it open. Grace clicked the left button of the mouse, and the screen immediately sprang to life, revealing a login box for her username and password. Carefully, she entered the combination of letters and numbers she'd been given and hit *Enter*. Within seconds, she was in.

The blue screen was blank apart from a flashing green box in the top right corner. Grace clicked on it. As soon as she did, a list of dates appeared down the left side of the screen, ranging from 1965 to 1970. She selected the first of them – Friday 1st January 1965. The front page of a newspaper immediately opened on the screen. It was like no newspaper she'd ever seen. It had the usual name banner at the top and a few small pictures, but the rest was just a mass of words. Eight narrow columns of teeny, tiny words. She sighed. This was going to take ages.

Grace zoomed in on the page and instantly felt better. The whole of the first page was adverts for shops and shows – no need to read that. The second page covered a variety of topics – notices from the magistrate's court, letters, more adverts and the occasional reported event.

Luckily, each individual article had a small heading. It was going to be easier than she'd initially thought.

8th January, 15th January, 22nd January, 29th January – nothing. The same for February, March, April, May, June, July, August, September, October, November and December.

Grace checked her watch. 12:45.

She stretched and looked around. The top floor of the library was now empty apart from her. She'd been so engrossed in the newspapers she hadn't even noticed the old man leave. Sighing, she turned back to the screen. She'd been looking at the newspapers for two hours and had only covered one year. With renewed determination, she clicked open the next paper.

'Hey, Grace!'

Grace looked up with a start. 'Sorry, I was miles away,' she said, rolling her shoulders to ease out the knots.

Abeer sat down on the chair next to her. 'Must be interesting stuff,' he said, squinting at the screen.

'Not really. Looking for a needle in a haystack more like it,' Grace replied. She glanced behind him. 'No Anya?'

'No. Dad picked her up a while ago. Mum manages the library, and I've been helping her with some bits and pieces. She just asked me to check if 'the girl on the computers' was okay.' He smiled. 'I'm guessing she means you as you're the only person up here.'

'Yeah, I've been here a while,' she replied, rubbing her eyes.

Abeer glanced at his watch. 'Why don't you take a break and I'll carry on searching for you while I wait for Mum to finish up. You look like you could use it.'

Grace hesitated. It was 3pm and she hadn't eaten a thing since breakfast. She really could use some lunch.

'Okay. That'd be great. I'm looking for any mention of a girl called Olivia or Liv going missing. I'm up to …' She checked the screen. '… 29th March 1968.'

She stood up. 'I won't be long. And thanks again.' She picked up her purse off the desk and went in search of food.

Twenty minutes later, she was back.

'Any luck?' she asked as Abeer stood up from the desk and gestured for Grace to sit.

'Not a thing.' He stretched. 'Some good news and some bad news, though. Which do you want first?'

'Bad news.'

'Okay. The bad news is that Mum's ready to go, so I've got to leave you to it.'

'And the good news?'

'I think I can hear the good news walking up the stairs.' He grinned. 'See you in school,' he said, waving over his shoulder as he walked to the stairs. Seconds later, Suzy emerged, clutching a slip of paper in her hand.

'Abeer filled me in on where we're at … which is

nowhere ... so I got myself a login. Two pairs of eyes, half the time, right?' she said, sitting at the computer to Grace's right and logging on.

'Thanks, Suze. How'd the clothes shopping go? Was it as bad as you thought?'

'To start off with it was *so* bad! You should've seen the monstrosities Mum tried to get me to try on. There were frills, flowers, sequins – the works! It's like she's never met me!'

'So what're you going to wear to the wedding?'

'Well, *eventually* Mum listened to what I was saying and bought me an awesome midnight blue tux. She drew the line at me wearing my All Stars with it though. I swear she has no sense of style!'

Grace glanced at the pair of slightly scruffy, black and white high tops that were a permanent fixture on Suzy's feet. 'I think your mum might be right on this one!'

'Thanks for your support, friend!' Suzy quipped then turned back to the screen. 'Right, time to get back to it. What date do you want me to start on?'

'You finish off 1968 and I'll take 1969,' Grace said.

Suzy quickly brought up the next set of articles. 'Come on, Liv, where are you?' she muttered at the screen.

Grace stretched her arms above her head, her shoulders creaking in protest, and went back to work.

They worked in silence, each focusing all of their attention on the screen in front of them until Grace gasped.

'Suze! I … I think I've found her!' She pointed at the screen. 'See here. *Missing Schoolgirl. Local girl Olivia Montague, 14, was reported missing by her parents yesterday after she failed to arrive at the house of a friend. Olivia left her parents' house, Barrington Grange, at 3:25pm but failed to arrive at her destination. Olivia is approximately 5 feet 4 inches tall, has a blonde bob and was last seen wearing a blue dress. If you see her, you can contact the family or local police.* This is her! It *must* be! The Liv in my visions had a blonde bob *and* she was wearing a blue dress!'

'Quick, pull up the next week's paper,' Suzy said,

her voice filled with excitement.

Grace clicked back to the list of dates and selected the next one down. 15th August 1969. She didn't so much as glance at the first page and clicked straight to the fourth column on the second page. 'Here it is again. *Missing girl, Olivia Montague still not found.*' She clicked into the following week's edition, and the next, and both featured reports of the missing girl but then nothing. Nothing to say she was still missing. Nothing to say she had been found.

'They never found her, did they?' Grace whispered, flopping back into her chair. 'Her body was never found, and now it's up to me to find her.'

'Hang on. You want to find a dead body and dig it up?' Suzy asked doubtfully.

'I have to, don't I? That's what these visions are – Liv asking me for help.'

'Well yeah ... but ...' Suzy pulled a face. She looked green. 'Remember when we found Mrs Peel's rabbit that had been eaten by a fox, and we took it back to her?' Grace nodded. She'd wrapped poor Mr Fluffles in her school jumper, and Suzy had thrown up all the way home. 'Well, Liv is going to be a lot bigger than a rabbit.'

'I know, but her killer is a free man. If we find Liv's body, the police could gather enough evidence to arrest him and lock him up. Who knows, he could have killed other girls, or who's to say he's not out there somewhere about to murder someone else? We can't ignore this.'

Suzy let out a shaky breath. 'So, we're really doing this?'

Grace nodded. 'I can't believe it either, but yes. I think we have to.'

CHAPTER 7

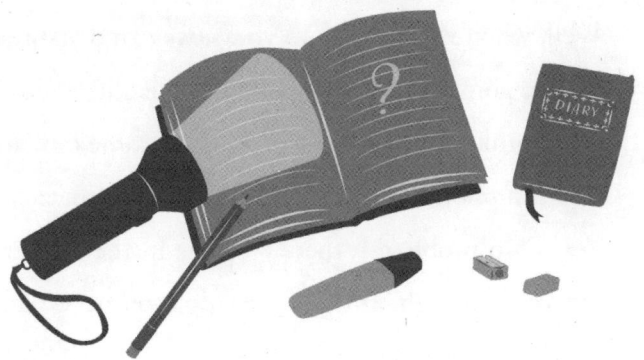

Grace and Suzy logged out of the computers, thanked the librarian and headed back to Grace's house.

'Okay, so we know who the girl in your vision was, who her parents were and where she lived.' Suzy counted off the points on her fingers as she said them. 'That's pretty good for a day's work I'd say.' She smiled over at Grace, who was frowning. 'Okay, what's wrong?'

'No, you're right. It's great we know who she is and

all the rest, but where do we go from here? It feels like we're no closer to finding out what happened to Liv or knowing who the boy, Johnny, was,' Grace sighed.

'Well, when we get back to yours, we can work out what we're going to do next.' Suzy checked her watch. 'Do you think your mum'd mind if I get some food at yours? I can phone Dad and tell him I'll be home late.'

'Yeah. No problem – there's a pizza in the freezer. I warn you, though. It's got pineapple on it.' Grace grinned as her friend pulled a face.

'You, Grace Yi, are officially a freak.'

'Well ... if you don't want my pizza ...' Grace laughed.

'Now, I didn't say that, did I?'

When they arrived at her house, Grace turned the oven on, setting the timer for ten minutes for it to heat up. 'Right, let's go upstairs,' she said, and Suzy followed her to her bedroom. Once inside, Grace pulled the notepad and pen out of her bag and sat on the bed next to Suzy.

'So, how are we going to find out more about Liv? Did you manage to work out anything from the diary that'll help us?' Grace asked as she wrote Liv in the middle of a clean page and drew a bubble around it.

'Not yet. But I'll keep trying. In the meantime, we do know she was from a wealthy family, so she probably went to a private school. It should be easy to find out what schools were around back then,' Suzy said as Grace scribbled notes. 'And we know who her family are and where they lived, so we could visit them.'

'Hmmm ... I'm not sure about that. What would we say to them?' Grace asked, writing it down anyway.

'Yeah, good point. Maybe we could try and find some of her friends once we know where she went to school?'

'I'd be happier doing that. We can always make up a school project to justify why we're asking questions,' Grace agreed.

Beep, beep. Beep, beep.

'I'll go and sort the pizza. You turn on my laptop and start researching private schools from the 1960s,' Grace

said as she leapt off the bed and hurried to the kitchen.

'So, what've you found?' Grace asked, placing the pizza on the desk. She pulled a slice off and bounced down next to Suzy.

'Thanks.' Suzy grabbed a piece, pulling off the pieces of pineapple before taking a bite. 'Mmmm,' she sighed, closing her eyes.

'So?' Grace prompted.

'Yes, right,' Suzy mumbled through a mouthful of pizza. 'There are a few schools she could have gone to. City High School for Girls, Clover Street Secondary Modern, Broadmead Secondary, Christleton, Charles King Secondary School for Girls and Duchesse School. Duchesse is the only private school, so I reckon we start there if Liv was rich.'

'Okay.' Grace pulled the laptop away from Suzy so her friend would be free to eat. She typed in Duchesse School and hit enter. The school's website appeared on the screen and Grace clicked through the various menus to try to find any information from the 1960s, but it was all current. 'Argh, nothing!' She punched at the keys to return to the search engine. 'Okay, so not their website. How about Duchesse School 1960s … bingo! There's a school magazine. It's a long shot, but it might mention her? What was the date of the newspaper with the missing report?'

Suzy flicked back through the notepad, her finger running down the page.

'8th August 1969.'

'Right, so if she was 14 then, she would have started secondary school at 11, which would be 1966. So, we should start looking at the magazines from that time and keep a lookout for any mention of her name,' Grace said, opening the first year. Suzy looked over her shoulder as she scanned lists of actors in the school's annual performance, prize recipients and piano recital awards.

'There!' Suzy almost shouted, pointing at the list of hockey 1st team players.

Grace leant closer. 'Good spot! Right, read me the names of her teammates. They might know something about the mysterious Johnny.'

'Okay; Sarah Whittingstock, Gillian Meadows, Sally Meade, Joan Freeman, Victoria Bussell, Mary Goodyear, Harriet Simms, Katherine Jones and Georgina May. Do you need me to repeat any?'

Grace read back the names she'd written as Suzy checked them against those on screen. 'Perfect,' Suzy said when she'd finished. She yawned and looked at her watch. 'Wow, it's 8 o'clock. I'd better be getting home.' She headed for the door, texting her dad as she went. 'We're going out for the day tomorrow, but I'll see you for school on Monday, yeah?'

'Yeah.' Grace watched as her best friend walked down the path. 'Hey, Suze!' she called after her. 'It's late. Go to your window to let me know you got back okay.'

Suzy gave her a thumbs up and continued down the road.

Grace hurried back upstairs, stood by her bedroom window and waited. Suzy's house was directly behind

Grace's, and their bedroom windows were almost opposite each other. A few years ago, they'd even learnt Morse code so they could chat into the night when they should have been asleep. It had worked perfectly until Suzy's dad had gone into the bathroom one night and noticed the flickering lights.

In no time, Suzy's bedroom light came on and she waved over at Grace before closing her bedroom curtains. Satisfied her friend was okay, Grace sat back down at her computer and looked at the list of names they'd made earlier.

Some of them must still live locally, she thought, waking up her laptop again.

She typed in Telephone Directory and pulled up the BT web page. There was no listing for Whittingstock, Meadows or Mead, but there was a J Freeman listed. She scribbled down the address and telephone number and added a question mark next to it – could this J Freeman be Joan Freeman? She worked through the next names on the list. No Bussell nor Goodyear, a P Simms but not H Simms and 13 K Joneses. Her pen hovered over the pad. 13 was a lot to check. She took a screen print and saved it to the desktop before typing the final name.

'Yes!' Grace cried out. On the screen was not just a G May, but a Georgina May. She wrote down the details and circled them twice. This person was definitely the most likely to be one of Liv's teammates.

Grace grabbed her phone, opened Facebook and searched for Georgina May. A few were listed but none of them looked to be in their 60s. She closed Facebook and brought up a map instead. After checking the details she'd written down, Grace typed in Georgina's address and clicked on *Directions*. A blue line appeared on the map, and Grace followed it with her finger. It was pretty close. She'd be able to walk it in less than an hour.

She smiled as she put her phone on charge – she'd need it for her walk to Georgina's tomorrow.

CHAPTER 8

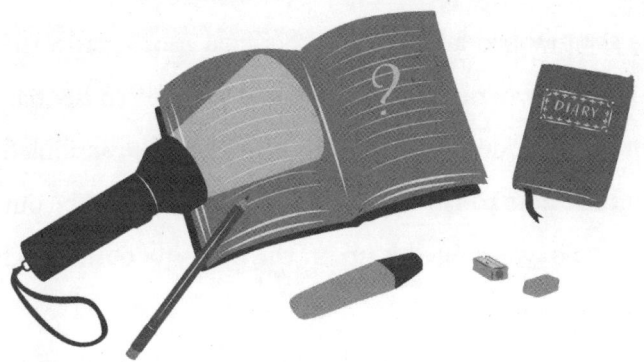

Grace leapt out of bed the second her alarm went off. Usually, she wouldn't dream of being out of bed at 8:30 on a Sunday morning, but this was a special case.

She hastily brushed her teeth while texting Suzy with her other hand to let her know where she was going and arranging to text her again when she left. There was no way she was going to tell her mum, but she knew that she should tell *somebody* what she was up to. Hopping on one leg, she pulled on yesterday's jeans and grabbed a fresh t-shirt out of a drawer. She glanced out of the window. It looked sunny but cool, so she grabbed a hoodie and her coat too. Finally, she unplugged her phone, put the pad and pen in her bag and jogged downstairs. Before she left, she scribbled a quick note to her mum to let her know she'd be out for the day, propped it up on the kitchen counter and left the house.

She'd been right, despite the sunshine, a chill wind cut through her thin cotton top, and she quickly pulled on the hoodie and tucked her hands inside the cuffs.

Grace had lived in the same house all her life and knew the local roads well, so she was able to follow the map in her head for most of the way. When she passed the local sports centre, she knew she was getting close to her destination and pulled out her phone to check the exact location of the house. It wasn't far.

Holding the phone in front of her, Grace followed the route until she'd reached the road she was looking for – Belvedere Close. The road was a cul-de-sac of garden-fronted stone cottages, each with a wooden picket fence separating it from the pavement. Most had house numbers on the garden gate or front door, and Grace glanced to the house on her left as she passed. Number 1.

She slipped her phone into the back pocket of her jeans then pulled the pad out of her bag to check which house she needed. Number 63.

Grace continued up the road and noticed that, unlike her road where the odd numbers were one side of the road and even on the other, the house numbers on Belvedere Close were consecutive. Uncertain of which side of the road number 63 would be on, she checked the number of the house opposite. Number 82. She crossed the road, following the numbers as they counted down, and in no time, she reached 63.

Grace's heart beat a rapid tattoo as she stepped towards the gate at the front.

The house itself was a beautiful stone cottage with pink roses climbing either side of the dark blue front door. The windows were double-glazed, but the panes of glass were cut into diamonds to look like the original leaded windows. Each had a window box in front of it, full of brightly coloured flowers. It was, quite possibly, the most beautiful house Grace had ever seen. She reached out to open the small wrought iron garden gate and hesitated.

What am I going to say? She kicked herself. What was she thinking just coming straight here? Why didn't she phone ahead?

Sighing, she let go of the gate and turned to walk away.

'Can I help you?'

Grace turned back to see a man in brown corduroy trousers, checked shirt and moss green cardigan standing in the doorway. He smiled as he stepped into the front garden.

'I, er, I'm looking for Georgina May,' Grace stammered. 'Does she live here?'

'Why yes, she does,' he replied. 'She's not in at the moment though. Can I help you?'

Grace's face fell. She'd come all this way for nothing.

'No, it's okay. It's Georgina I need to speak to. It's about Duchesse School ... or about someone who went there with her, anyway. I'll come back another time.' Grace turned to leave.

'Hey ... I might be able to help you. I'm her brother. You look like you've walked here – at least let me get you a drink and you can tell me what you'd like to know.'

Grace hesitated. Going into a lady's house was one thing, but going into a house with a strange man was something else.

'Don't worry, I won't bite.' The man smiled, stepping to the side of the doorway to allow her room to enter.

He certainly looked friendly enough. Plus, Suzy knew where she was and would be waiting for her text. Satisfied the likelihood that he was a serial killer was slim, she thanked him and entered the house.

The inside was just as perfect as the outside, with polished oak floors, cream walls and two well-used brown leather sofas either side of a large stone fireplace.

'Your house is lovely, Mr May,' Grace said as she took the seat offered to her.

'You can call me Frank, my dear. And you are?'

'Oh, sorry, I'm Grace. I hope you don't mind me calling round without phoning first.'

'Not at all,' Frank replied, taking a seat on the sofa opposite. 'Now, you said you wanted to ask Georgie about a girl she went to school with.' Grace nodded. 'There were always girls at our house from this club or that club, so I might be able to help. Who is it you're interested in?'

'It was a girl Georgina was on the hockey team with, Olivia Montague – but she might have gone by Liv,' Grace said.

Surprise briefly registered on Frank's face but was gone so quickly Grace wasn't sure if she'd imagined it. 'Let me see … Olivia Montague … it was such a long time ago, but I'm sure that name is familiar.' He paused.

'She may have left the school suddenly – if that helps?' Grace added.

'Oh yes. I remember now. She and my sister were friends back in the day … until she disappeared of course. My sister was heartbroken that Liv took off like that without even telling her where she was going.' He shook his head at the memory.

'So, your sister thought she'd run away?' Grace asked.

'Yes, well, *everyone* did. She was always one for adventure was Liv, and she didn't always get the chance with that family of hers. We thought she must have gone to London to become a model – she'd always talked about it you see, but we never thought she'd actually do it.'

'Do you think she ran off by herself? Or could she have gone with a boyfriend?' Grace pressed.

Frank shifted in his seat. 'Oh, I don't think she had a boyfriend. Not a steady one anyway. No. If she ran away, she did it by herself.' He stood up and stepped towards the living room door. 'Anyway, if you'll excuse me, I've got a few errands to run this morning …'

Grace took the hint and stood up. Her coat tumbled off her knee and onto the floor. 'Oh, of course,' she said, bending to pick it up. 'Could I just ask one more question, though?'

Frank didn't reply. He was frozen to the spot, his eyes fixed on the fallen coat.

'Mr May? Are you okay?' Grace asked.

Frank blinked a few times and almost seemed surprised to see Grace stood in his living room.

'Ah yes. I'm fine. I just had a funny turn. It happens sometimes if I stand up too quickly,' he replied, his eyes flicking back to the coat before he continued to the front door. 'Now, what was it you wanted to ask?'

'Do you remember anyone who lived around here at the time called Johnny? He'd have been older than Olivia?'

'Let me see,' he said, glancing away from Grace. 'Johnny ... Johnny ... no. No, I don't think I remember anyone of that name.' He paused and cleared his throat. 'And what *is* your interest in Olivia Montague?'

'Her name just came up while I was working on a school project, that's all.' She smiled and walked through the front door. As she stepped outside, Frank passed her a piece of paper and a pen.

'Why don't you write down your name and telephone

number and I'll get Georgie to give you a call when she gets back? She'll be able to tell you much more than me.'

Grace hesitated, certain that Frank wasn't telling her everything but unsure why. Then she took the paper and wrote down her details. After all, where was the harm in giving a phone number? 'Thank you,' she said, handing back the items to Frank then walking down the garden path. As she closed the gate behind her, she looked back at the house.

Frank was still in the doorway, watching her with a strange expression on his face.

CHAPTER 9

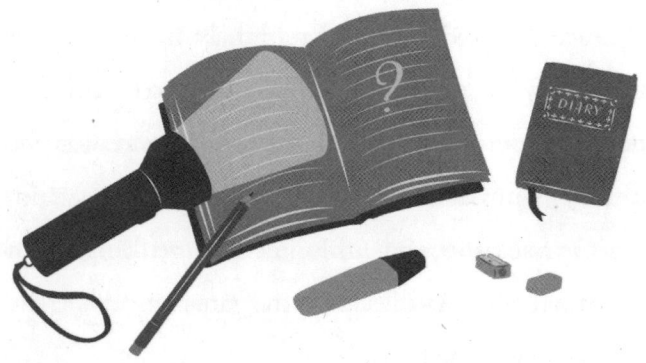

Once he was sure she'd gone, Frank closed the front door and leant against it.

The girl had Liv's old coat with her. The coat he'd kept in his allotment shed all those years. What were the chances?

Frank wiped his hand down his face.

He'd known he should have got rid of the coat years ago. He'd had plenty of opportunities, but no. He'd waited until the allotment site was bought by a property developer, *forcing him to empty it.*

Stupid!

He'd have to call Johnny, that much was certain, but no way would he be telling him about the coat. Or the bike.

He walked back through to the living room, picked up his mobile from on top of a cupboard next to the fireplace and selected a number from his contacts. He raked his hand through his hair as it rang out.

'Yes?'

'It's me, Frank. I thought you should know. A girl's been round asking questions about Olivia Montague,' Frank said.

'Who is she? Do we need to be concerned?'

'No. She's just a local schoolgirl doing a project for school. She was after Georgie, but luckily she wasn't here.'

'Okay, just make sure they never get to meet. Oh, and Frank?'

'Yes?'

'Have someone watch this girl. We don't want her getting too nosy. If she does, she could make things

difficult. For both of us.'

The line went dead.

Frank put the phone down and tucked Grace's details into the back pocket of his trousers before walking to the understairs cupboard. He pulled out a small lockbox, then reached inside his shirt to pull out a fine gold chain with a key dangling from it. It slid smoothly into the lock and the lid sprang open. The box contained only two items. A card and a photo. He picked up the photo and sighed.

He didn't have a choice.

He'd have to sort the girl.

Frank locked the box and hid it away before making another call. This one was picked up on the first ring.

'Yeah?'

'I've got a job for you ...'

CHAPTER 10

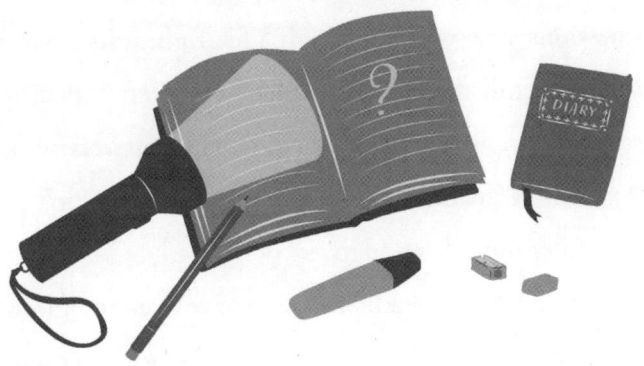

Grace sent a quick text to Suzy as soon as she was out of sight.

> GEORGINA NOT IN. SAW BRO INSTEAD BUT COULDN'T HELP. THINKS LIV RAN AWAY 2B A MODEL. DIDN'T KNOW ABOUT ANY BF. LEFT NUMBER 4 SIS 2 CALL IN CASE SHE KNOWS MORE. C U TOMORROW. X

She tucked her phone back in her pocket and ran through the conversation with Frank May. He'd been the perfect gentleman and had answered all of her questions, but something hadn't felt right. His answers seemed kind of rehearsed, like he'd been expecting someone to ask them and he'd got his answers ready. And when she'd asked about Johnny, he couldn't get rid of her quickly enough.

She shook her head. She must have been imagining it. But still ... the feeling that something wasn't quite right just wouldn't go away.

When Grace got home, she raced up to her bedroom and turned on her laptop. She took the notepad out of her bag and rechecked the list of names until she found the other possibility that she'd noted earlier. There it was. J Freeman with a question mark. *How am I going to find out if you're Joan?*

She tried typing Joan Freeman, Chesterford into Google, but nothing useful came up. 192.com drew a blank, as did LinkedIn and Facebook. Next, she tried the address 49 Banks Crescent, Chesterford.

Her heart skipped a beat when a planning application popped up on the screen. She clicked on the link and held her breath as she waited for the page to appear. A table of information flashed up – dates of applications, what had been applied for, reference numbers, status and all sorts of things she didn't understand. She moved the mouse over the screen until the cursor changed to a hand icon and then clicked again. It was an application for a new boiler. She clicked again to access the details and her heart sank. There were no details at all about the applicant, just confirmation that the application had been successful.

Grace drummed her fingers on the keyboard. What next? Joan Freeman Duchesse? Nothing. Joan Freeman hockey? Nothing.

'This is no use!' she huffed, slamming the laptop closed.

She looked at her pad again instead. There was a phone number. Maybe she should call? But what would she say? *Are you Joan Freeman?* No. She couldn't do that. A text then. That was it! She carefully keyed in the number and typed out a brief message.

DEAR MISS FREEMAN,
YOU DON'T KNOW ME BUT I'M DOING SOME RESEARCH ABOUT THE HOCKEY TEAM AT DUCHESSE SCHOOL IN 1969. I'VE COME ACROSS THE NAME JOAN FREEMAN AND WAS WONDERING IF THAT IS YOU? IF IT IS, I WOULD LOVE TO BE ABLE TO SPEAK TO YOU FOR A RESEARCH PAPER FOR SCHOOL. PLEASE COULD YOU TEXT ME BACK ON THIS NUMBER. THANK YOU,
GRACE YI

She read over the message and pressed send. All she could do now was wait.

Or was it?

Grace looked over at the wardrobe.

Maybe the coat could help her?

She hurried over, swung open the doors and lifted the coat off its hanger. She hesitated slightly before putting it on – she *had* promised Suzy she wouldn't wear it without her – but what was the worst that could happen? She slipped the coat on, sat on her bed and waited.

Nothing happened.

She picked up a book off her bedside table and read for a while.

Still nothing happened. Needing to do *something*, Grace went downstairs for a drink. Her mum walked out of the office just as she reached the bottom step.

'Oh Grace, I'm just going to start cooking dinner,' her mum said. 'How does lasagne sound?'

'Great. Garlic bread?'

'Of course.' Her mum smiled. 'Hey, is that a new coat?'

'Yeah, I got it from a charity shop on the high street.'

'It really suits you,' her mum said before going into the kitchen. Grace followed her in.

'Mum?'

'Hmmm?'

'Do you believe in ghosts? Or in spirits possessing

things?' she asked, sitting at the counter.

'Uh, no. Why?'

'Oh nothing. Some of the kids at school watched a film about a girl who got visions when she wore a hat. They said it was based on a true story.'

'I think they were pulling your leg, love.' She straightened up from putting the lasagne in the oven and programmed the timer. 'I've got some more work to do now, so could you listen out for the buzzer and give me a shout when it's done?' She walked out of the room without waiting for a reply.

Great, Grace thought. *Just what I want to be doing.* She pulled off her coat, sat at the counter and thought about all of the things she had to tell Suzy in the morning.

When the doorbell buzzed at 8:30am, Grace was ready and waiting in the hallway and immediately yanked open the door.

'Bye, Mum!' she called over her shoulder before dashing out of the house.

'So? Give me all the details!' Suzy blurted out as soon as Grace had closed the door behind them.

Grace filled her in on everything that had happened the day before and her doubts about Frank May.

'Yeah. I can see why you're a bit …' she wiggled her hand, 'about him. It does sound like he had an answer for everything, bearing in mind it all happened such a long time ago. Hopefully, his sister will call back soon so you can get it straight from the horse's mouth.'

'Yeah. I've texted the J Freeman from our search too. I tried Googling her, but I couldn't find anything to show if she is Joan Freeman, so I've asked her to text me back.'

'So now we just have to wait?' Suzy asked.

'Yep. Now we wait.'

At 2:45pm, Grace's phone vibrated in her pocket. She

glanced around.

She was in geography class and everyone else had their head down making notes, so she *might* be able to get away with a quick look. She slowly reached into her pocket and glanced around once more. No one was watching. She pinched the top of her phone between her thumb and forefinger and gently pulled, all the while pretending to make notes with her right hand.

'Hey, Grace. What page do we read up to?' Abeer whispered, leaning over from his desk. Grace froze and turned to look at him.

'Oh, um, page 35 I think,' she stammered, certain he'd have noticed what she was doing.

'Thanks!' he grinned, brushing a stray strand of dark hair out of his eyes before turning back to his work.

That was close!

She paused, waiting until she was sure that Abeer wouldn't turn around again, but he seemed engrossed in his work. She quickly yanked the phone the last few centimetres out of her pocket and whipped it around under the desk in front of her.

Her heart hammered in her chest. She'd done it! Now all she needed to do was take a look at the screen to see who the message was from. She looked around again, but Mr Stewart looked up at the same time and caught her eye. Grace pushed down the panic that threatened to give her away and quickly looked back down at her work. Had he seen her? She held her breath, listening for any sign she'd been caught but all was quiet. After quickly checking Mr Stewart was engrossed in his marking, Grace risked a glance at the screen.

HI GRACE. YOU'RE RIGHT, I AM …

and that was all that showed without unlocking the phone.

'Is it an important message?'

Grace almost jumped out of her chair. She spun around and Abeer smiled, nodding over at her phone.

'Um, yeah. It is.'

'Okay,' he replied and stood up.

Grace panicked and whipped the phone back under

the table, but Abeer just winked at her and walked towards Mr Stewart's desk. She sank down low in her chair. She was in for it now.

'Sir? I'm looking at page 34 and I don't quite understand the part about lateral moraines also being supraglacial moraines. If you look at this diagram ...' Abeer placed the textbook on the teacher's desk and positioned himself directly between Mr Stewart and Grace. 'It shows lateral moraines are formed at the outside of ...'

Grace stopped listening and took the opportunity given to her. She unlocked the screen and tapped on the message.

HI GRACE, YOU'RE RIGHT, I AM JOAN FREEMAN FROM DUCHESSE. I'M MEETING MY DAUGHTER AT THE ROSE CAFE ON THE HIGH STREET LATER – DO YOU KNOW IT? – IF YOU WANT TO MEET YOU COULD COME FOR 4PM? IT'S NOT EVERY DAY I GET TO CHAT ABOUT THE OLD DAYS! SEE YOU LATER. JOAN

It *was* Joan from the hockey team! Grace typed a quick reply:

GREAT. I'LL SEE YOU AT 4. GRACE

She pressed send and thrust the phone back into her pocket just as Abeer said, 'Thanks, Mr Stewart. That makes much more sense.' He picked up his textbook and walked back to his seat. When his eyes met hers, Grace smiled and mouthed *thank you*. He smiled back, then sat down and continued with his notes.

When the bell rang for the end of the lesson, Grace grabbed her books and stuffed them in her bag before hurrying out of the classroom.

'Excuse me … excuse me … can I just squeeze past? … ah, made it!' Abeer fell into step beside Grace. 'You're in a hurry to get out of here.'

'Yeah, I'm meeting someone,' Grace replied.

'Ah, the mysterious text message.' Abeer let the sentence hang, but Grace didn't take the bait.

'Look, I've really got to get going. I'll see you

tomorrow,' she said, checking the time on her phone and hurrying out of the school building.

CHAPTER 11

Grace arrived at the coffee shop fifteen minutes early, and it wasn't at all what she'd expected from the name.

She'd pictured Rose Café as having pine tables and chairs, checked tablecloths and floral wallpaper. But inside, the walls were exposed brick and lined with black and white photos of celebrities. Instead of tables and chairs, there were sofas, armchairs and coffee tables, each with a different kind of lamp dangling from the ceiling above. Chatter and laughter from the occupied seats filled the air, and Grace didn't think she'd ever been in anywhere as wonderful before.

She walked across the café to a long copper counter that stretched the length of the room. At one end was a kitchen area with panini presses and bread ovens, and at the other was the hot drink station. In between was a huge selection of cakes and pastries, each protected by a large glass dome. Grace cursed herself for not bringing more money.

'Can I help you?' the girl behind the counter asked.

Grace looked longingly at the cakes but said, 'Just a hot chocolate, please.'

'Would you like whipped cream?'

Grace checked the prices on the board. She could just about afford the extra cost. 'Yes, please.'

The assistant put her order through the till and Grace handed over the money.

'Won't be long,' the girl said, clipping Grace's order slip onto a board next to the hot drink machines.

While she waited for her hot chocolate, Grace looked

around the room and considered where she should sit. There was a pair of armchairs available right by the door. If she sat there, she would see Joan straight away when she arrived … or would she? It struck her then that she didn't have a clue what Joan looked like, and Joan didn't know what she looked like either. Maybe she was in the café already?

Grace swept her eyes over the seated customers, looking for a lady in her 60s who was sitting alone, but no one matched that description. Satisfied she hadn't arrived yet, she continued to deliberate where to sit. The seats by the door *would* be good for visibility but weren't very private with everyone walking past. All the available sofas were facing away from the door, so they wouldn't do. There was only one decent prospect – a pair of armchairs by themselves to the right of the counter, facing the door. Once her drink was ready, she sat down and waited.

At exactly 4pm, a lady who looked to be about the right age entered the café. She was tall and slender with a shoulder-length platinum bob and wore a cream blouse and slim-fitting jeans. She hesitated for a moment by the door, scanning the room. Spotting Grace, she raised an eyebrow and Grace smiled in return. She walked over, oozing confidence despite this being an unusual meeting.

'Grace?' she asked when she reached her table.

Grace stood and held out her hand. 'Yes, are you Joan?'

'Yes, I am. Lovely to meet you, Grace,' Joan replied, shaking her hand. 'I'll just leave my things here and go and get a cuppa, and then we can chat about the good old days at Duchesse. Won't be a mo.'

She walked away to the counter and returned a few moments later, drink in hand, and took the seat opposite Grace.

'So, Duchesse, eh? It's been a long time. To be honest, I was quite surprised to get your message. What's your project on?'

'Um, well, originally, we were looking at the history of local schools. Duchesse is the oldest in the area, so it seemed a good idea to start there. But while we were doing our research, we came across the story of a girl who went missing and, well, we just wanted to know more about her.'

'Ah, yes. Liv.' Joan took a sip of her tea. 'Terrible really.'

'What do you mean?' Grace asked.

'Well, no one really knew what happened to her. They *said* she'd run off to London to become a model, but she wouldn't have done that without telling anyone. You see, Liv was ... effervescent. If something exciting was going to happen, she wouldn't have been able to keep it to herself and would at least have told Georgie. They were best friends, you see.'

'Is that Georgina May?'

Joan looked slightly taken aback. 'My, you have done your research! Have you spoken to her yet? She'd be the best person to speak to about Liv.'

'I went round to her house yesterday but she was out, so I spoke to her brother, Frank. He didn't really know anything either.'

'Hmmm, yes. Well, I'll just say Frank isn't the best person to speak to about Liv. He–'

'Mum! Here you are!' A young woman in an apron engulfed Joan in a hug before noticing Grace. 'Oh, I'm sorry, I'm interrupting you!'

Joan turned to Grace with a smile. 'Grace, this is my daughter, Phoebe. She owns Rose Café and bakes the best cakes in town, even if I do say so myself!'

'Mum! Grace is already here – she doesn't need the sales pitch!' Phoebe joked, tucking a stray tendril of curly blonde hair back into her ponytail.

Not wanting to interrupt Joan's meeting with her daughter, Grace stood up. 'Well, it's been lovely to meet both of you. Thanks for agreeing to talk to me. I'll leave you two alone now.'

'And lovely to meet you too, my dear. I'll send Georgie a message to let her know you'd like to speak to her. I'm sure she'll be in touch.'

Grace smiled her thanks and put on her coat.

'My goodness!' Joan exclaimed. 'You won't know this, but Liv had a coat just like that one. How incredible! Her parents gave it to her for her 14th birthday, and she barely left the house without it. She really did love that coat.' Joan seemed lost in her memories for a moment but then looked at Grace and smiled. 'I think, young lady, you are meant to find out what happened to Liv, and I wish you the best of luck.'

I think so too – Liv has made sure of that, Grace thought, but simply smiled again and weaved her way back between the now-filled tables to the door.

The moment she left the café, Grace shivered involuntarily and stopped in her tracks. She couldn't put her finger on it, but something didn't feel right.

Frowning, she glanced around but couldn't see anything that would have made the hairs stand up on the back of her neck. Why did she feel so anxious all of a sudden?

Grace shook the feeling off and had just turned to walk home when she saw a man sitting in a silver car across the road from the café.

She'd noticed the same man sitting in the car half an hour earlier when she'd arrived too. That in itself wouldn't have been strange. It was the fact that both times she'd seen him, he wasn't doing *anything*. Not reading, nor on his phone, nor listening to music. And she was pretty sure he'd been watching her when she'd walked out of the café, but now he was just staring straight ahead.

Grace kept watching him for a few moments more, but he didn't look her way once. *Stop being paranoid, Grace*, she thought to herself and continued home. When she reached the street corner to turn right, she glanced over her shoulder towards the car then quickly turned away.

The driver was looking straight at her.

CHAPTER 12

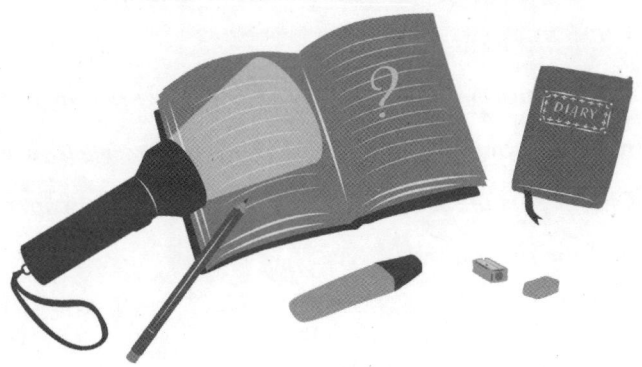

He watched her until she'd turned the corner and walked out of sight. Then he picked up his mobile and selected a number. The call was answered on the first ring.

'You've got news?' Frank asked immediately.

'Yeah, the girl has met with Joan Freeman. She's just left her now.'

The phone fell silent. He knew better than to say anything.

'That's ... inconvenient. Has she been in touch with

my sister yet?'

'Not that I've seen.'

'Good. Keep watching and keep me updated.'

The line went dead.

The driver put his mobile on the seat next to him and drove back to Grace's house, making sure to park in a different part of the street to where he'd parked to watch her house that morning.

CHAPTER 13

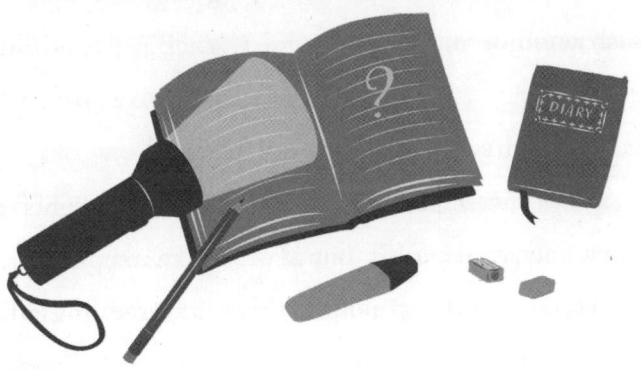

Instead of going straight home, Grace went round to Suzy's house to fill her in on the meeting with Joan. When she arrived, she ignored the brass doorbell to the left of the front door and took out her phone.

I'M HERE. LET ME IN. X

The bell hadn't worked for as long as Grace had known Suzy, and with Suzy's bedroom being in the attic, a text was usually the only way to get in. There was a groan of wood on wood from above, and Grace looked up to see her friend forcing open the warped sash window to her room. Suzy stuck her head out and waved.

'I'll be down now. Hang on!'

Suzy's footsteps thundered down the two flights of stairs and she emerged, out of breath, moments later.

'Hey,' Suzy said, stepping back into the house to let Grace in.

Grace was always taken aback by the sense of chaos in Suzy's house. Brightly coloured rugs and throws covered the floor and walls of the hallway, and the air was filled with the heavy scent of sandalwood. Each step of the long, straight staircase was painted a different colour and the banister had been removed, according to Suzy, to create a sense of openness and to allow spirits to move freely.

Grace followed Suzy upstairs, walking as close to the wall as possible. Suzy however, skipped up them oblivious to the sheer drop just to her right. When they finally got to Suzy's room, Grace relaxed. It was like a haven of calm after the maelstrom of the rest of the house. Suzy had kept it simple. Apart from the walls, which changed as frequently as she changed her hair colour, everything was white – the curtains, carpet, bedding and furniture. The walls were currently hot pink.

Suzy flopped on the bed.

'So, what happened with Joan?' she asked.

Grace put her bag on the floor before joining Suzy.

'There's not much to tell,' she sighed. 'Joan was really nice, but she couldn't tell me anything I didn't already know from speaking to Frank, though I got the impression she didn't like Frank much. She made me think we couldn't trust what he told us … which wasn't much anyway, so I guess it doesn't really matter. She's texted Georgina May to get in touch, so that was one good thing to come out of it.'

'Well, you've made some progress,' Suzy said. 'You've managed to cross Joan Freeman off your list of people to speak to. That's something.'

'I guess so. It's just so frustrating having to wait – ooh, speaking of waiting. The strangest thing happened when I left the café.'

Suzy sat up straighter, noticing the tension in her friend's voice.

'What?'

'It's probably nothing, but I could have sworn that a man in a car parked opposite the café was watching me.'

'Why d'you say that? If he was parked, couldn't he have been waiting for someone?'

'I know. It just felt … I don't know … odd.'

'I think this Liv thing is getting to you. I'm sure it's nothing to worry about. After all, why would anyone be watching you? If you do see him again, then that *would* be odd,' Suzy added.

'You're right. I'm being paranoid. Anyway, I'd better go. I told Mum I'd be home for dinner.'

'Okay, let me know if you hear from Georgina May.'

'Will do.' Grace picked up her bag and sidled back down the stairs and out of the house.

The first few times she'd visited all those years ago,

Suzy had always walked her to the front door. After a while, Suzy admitted it was a pain to have to go all the way down to go all the way back up again, so they'd agreed that Grace could make her own way out. She was amazed that her friend still bothered to let her in. One of these days she was sure that Suzy would figure out she could just chuck the front door keys out of the window so Grace could let herself in!

When she reached the end of Suzy's road, Grace turned right onto her street and froze.

Parked just up the road was a silver car. The same car that she'd seen outside the café. This was no coincidence. She was being watched. She was sure of it.

The car was facing the opposite direction to her, so she was pretty sure she hadn't been spotted, but how to get back home without being seen? Grace raced back to Suzy's house, firing off another text to her friend. Within seconds, the window opened.

'What did you forget?' Suzy shouted down.

'Nothing! You've got to get down here! The car from before is parked in my street!' Grace panted.

Without a word, Suzy disappeared from view, her thundering footsteps once again echoing through the house. In seconds, she yanked open the door, thrusting her feet into a pair of high tops.

'Show me,' she said, closing the door and hurrying down the path.

Grace led the way to the end of the road and stopped. The car was still there.

'Over there.' She pointed. 'The silver one over the road from my house.'

'You're sure it's the same one? There are lots of silver cars out there.'

'I'm certain. It's got the same blacked-out windows at the back and scratch along the side.'

Suzy took her phone out and took a picture. 'For insurance,' she said, turning the screen towards Grace.

'Okay, so we need to get you back home without being seen.' Suzy paused, thinking. 'I've got it. Why don't I go in your house and open the back door and garden gate? You go to the alley around the back and come in that way.'

Grace considered Suzy's plan, then nodded.

'Okay. Go. I'll see you in the house.' Grace thrust the keys at her friend and walked back to the alleyway that ran behind her house.

Suzy waved her phone in the air as she walked past the car, pretending to try to get a signal but all the while taking photos in the hope that one might capture the driver. She pocketed it once she was past.

When she arrived at the gate of Grace's house, she couldn't resist looking behind her. Her heart skipped a beat. The driver was definitely watching her.

She quickly walked up the path and fumbled the key into the lock, slamming the door behind her as soon as she was inside.

'Hi Grace,' Grace's mum called from her office. 'Dinner in five minutes!'

Suzy ignored her and rushed through the kitchen to unlock the back door then hurried into the garden. The garden gate hadn't been used for years and the bolt was rusted closed. Suzy tried yanking it open, but it wouldn't budge.

'What's going on?' Grace called from the alleyway.

'Just need to get the bolt open; it's rusted in place!' She tugged at one of the large stones that edged the lawn. 'Hang on, I think this'll do it!' she called before slamming the stone down on the bolt. Flakes of rust crumbled from the metal, and Suzy gave it another yank. This time it slid open with a loud creak of complaint. Immediately, the gate was tugged open from outside, and Grace quickly stepped into the garden, pulling the gate closed behind her and re-securing the bolt. The pair hurried into the house and locked the door behind them.

'Hey, girls. I didn't realise you were coming over to dinner, Suzy. I'm afraid I haven't made enough for you too, but I can put something in the microwave for you?' They spun around at the sound of Grace's mum's voice. She was pulling a casserole out of the oven.

'Oh, it's okay, Mrs Yi. I'm not staying,' Suzy replied. She tilted her head towards the door and looked meaningfully at Grace.

'I'll just see Suzy out. I'll be back in a sec, Mum.'

Grace and Suzy walked into the hall and stopped just inside the front door.

'I took some photos of the car with my phone, but I don't know if I caught anything,' Suzy whispered, pulling her phone out of her pocket. She tapped the screen and the first photo appeared. It was a dark blur. 'I clicked randomly so the driver wouldn't notice I was taking pictures, hopefully they're not all like this.' She swiped through dozens of photos then stopped. 'This one's pretty good.' She turned her phone towards Grace. On it was the silver car, slightly blurred, but they could just make out the face of the man in the driver's seat. 'I'll download it onto my laptop at home. Just in case.'

'Thanks, Suzy. And be careful.'

'You too.'

The friends hugged, and Suzy left the house. Grace shut the door and put the deadbolt on before returning to the kitchen for dinner.

'So, what have you been up to today? Anything interesting?' her mum asked as she passed a plate of food to Grace.

'Oh, nothing much. The usual really.'

'I don't know. You and Suzy always seem to be whispering about something these days. Is there a boy involved?' Her mum grinned.

'Mum! No, there's no boy!!!' Grace replied.

But there is a man, she added to herself.

CHAPTER 14

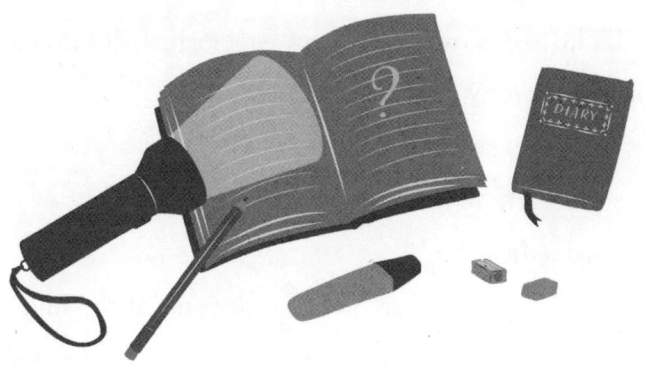

The next morning, Grace's alarm went off at 6:30. She raced to the landing window, which gave her an unrestricted view of the street.

The car was still there.

Grace ran back to her room and grabbed her phone from the bedside table. She pressed Suzy's number.

'Hi Grace, give me a sec – I just need to grab a towel.'

'Suzy? Suzy!' Grace hissed, but her friend had put the phone down. She could hear the slamming of drawers as Suzy hunted for a towel and then a rustle as she picked the phone back up.

'Right, I'm back.'

The words tumbled out of Grace's lips. 'It's the car, it's still here! What am I going to do?'

'Are you sure?'

'I'm certain. It's exactly the same one, and I can see someone inside it.'

There was a pause on the other end of the line as Suzy took in what Grace was telling her. 'Right. This is getting serious. You've got to call the police.'

'But what will I say? That there's a man sitting in his car? It's hardly enough for them to send someone round.'

'Hmmm. You're right. We'll need to make something up. Something that'd need acting on straight away. Leave it with me.' Suzy hung up.

Grace walked back to the landing window and glanced outside. She didn't know what she was expecting to have happened, but nothing had changed.

Sighing, she put on her dressing gown and went downstairs.

'You're up early,' her mum said, looking up from her newspaper as Grace entered the kitchen. 'Oh my goodness, what's the matter? You look like you've seen a ghost.' She rushed over to Grace.

'Nothing. I'm fine,' Grace replied. She tried to get to the fridge, but her mum blocked the way.

'Grace Yi, I'm your mum. I can tell when something's not right. Tell me.' She stood with her hands on her hips.

Grace sagged.

'It's probably nothing …'

'And …?'

'I think a man's been following me.'

Her mum's eyes widened. 'What?'

'He was parked opposite the café I went to after school yesterday, and he was still there when I left, and he was parked at the end of our road when I came back from Suzy's …'

'And?'

'And he's still there now. Sitting in his car.'

'Show me!' her mum hissed, furious.

'But–'

'Now!'

Grace slouched upstairs, her mum following close behind. When she got to the window, she pointed out the car.

'It's that one there.' She pointed. 'The silver one parked right at the end, on the opposite side of the road.'

'I see it. You wait here.'

Her mum stormed out of the room, her footsteps pounding on the stairs. Then there was a clink of keys and the front door slammed. Grace watched, horrified, as her mum strode down the street towards the car. When she reached it, she rapped on the window, and it was wound down a touch. Grace saw her mum jabbing her finger at the driver and pointing to their house before swivelling on her heels and striding back to the house. By the time she reached the gate, the car was already pulling away from the kerb. The front door slammed again.

Grace ran downstairs.

'What did you say?' she asked as she stepped off the final step.

'I gave him a piece of my mind. And told him that if I ever see him around here, or anywhere near you, again, then I will call the police. He drove off pretty sharpish after that.'

Grace skipped towards her mum and enveloped her in a huge hug.

'Thanks, Mum.'

'That's what mums are for.' She placed her hands on Grace's shoulders and held her at arm's length. 'Now, tell me. Why do you think he was watching you? You've not put your address online or anything have you? Or any other personal details? Or photos?'

'Of course not, Mum, we learnt all about internet safety in primary school!' Grace replied.

Her mum nodded but didn't move. 'If you're in trouble of any kind, you will tell me, won't you?' She searched Grace's eyes.

'Of course I will, Mum. Don't worry.'

'Alright. Make sure you do,' her mum replied. She glanced at the clock on the wall. 'Go on – you'd better get ready for school, or you'll be late.'

Grace smiled and turned to go upstairs.

'And you'd better give Suzy a call to let her know the man's sorted,' she said.

Grace looked incredulous. 'How–'

'The walls aren't as thick as you think.' Her mum raised her eyebrows and smiled. 'Now go!'

Grace didn't need telling twice. She shot up the stairs and called Suzy.

'Hey, Suze. It's sorted,' she said.

'Wow, that was quick! What happened?'

'Mum happened. She noticed I was looking worried and made me tell her why. Anyway, you should have seen her! She marched right over to the guy in the car and gave him hell. She told him if she ever sees him anywhere near me or the house again, she'll call the police. He had no choice but to drive away.'

'Wow,' Suzy breathed. 'I was planning all sorts of things we could do and none of them involved just marching on over there! Do you think he'll be back?'

'He'd be foolish to now.'

Both were silent for a while as they thought about

the events of the last few days.

Eventually, Grace said, 'I wonder why he was following me, though? Why's he interested in me?'

'Well, he's either a random stalker or it's something to do with Olivia Montague, and I think it's too much of a coincidence for it not to be about Liv,' Suzy answered.

Grace nodded. 'You could be right, but it's all so … crazy. Who would care that I was looking into a murder from decades ago?'

'Um, hello! The murderer?'

Grace blanched.

'You mean–' she paused. 'Hang on a minute. There's no way that guy was the murderer. He was only, like, 30 or something. The killer would be *much* older.'

Suzy thought about this for a moment.

'Okaaaay … then the murderer paid for someone to keep tabs on you, and they were reporting back to him.'

Grace opened her mouth and closed it again.

'As crazy as it sounds, you could be right. How will I know who's just minding their own business and who's watching me?'

'You don't. Just be on alert. Got to go, gonna be late for school if I don't get a move on.'

Grace checked the time. 'Argh … yes. See you in a bit!'

She hung up the phone and raced to the bathroom to brush her teeth.

CHAPTER 15

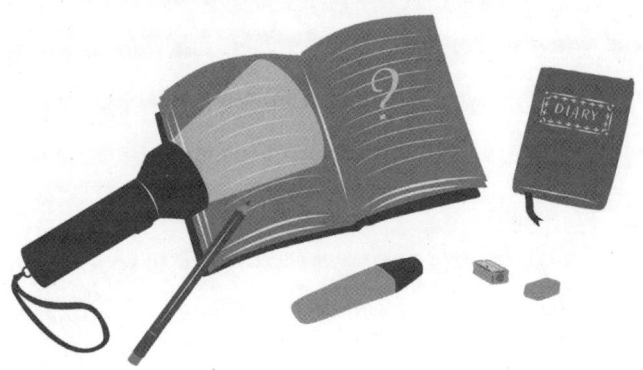

'Yes?' Frank answered.

'Bad news, she saw me.'

He sighed before saying, 'How do you know?'

'The girl's mum came over to my car this morning and told me to stay away or she'll call the cops.'

'Sloppy Jimmy. Very sloppy.'

'I was careful, Fr–'

'You were careful? You're done, Jimmy. I don't need you any more.' Frank slammed the phone down. Incompetent *idiot. How had he been complacent enough to let a 13-year-old girl spot him?*

He sat back and thought. Johnny wouldn't be happy he'd failed to have the girl watched, but Johnny was a man who knew people. And Frank knew he needed a pro.

He picked up the phone again.

'Yes?'

'Johnny, the girl's proving more difficult to keep tabs on than I thought. I need someone who knows what they're doing,' Frank said.

Johnny sighed. 'Do I have to do everything myself?' he asked. Frank stayed silent, knowing better than to answer. 'Check your phone. Call him and tell him the job's for me.'

Johnny hung up.

Frank checked his phone and called the number he'd been sent.

'Marco? Mr Bainbridge needs a job doing,' Frank said.

'Go on. I'm all ears.'

'We need you to watch someone … closely.'

'How closely?'

'Use everything you've got.'

CHAPTER 16

The doorbell rang, and Grace ran down the stairs.

'See you later, Mum!' she shouted.

'Take care!'

'Hey,' she greeted Suzy as she stepped out of the house. Then she looked at her friend. 'What have you done to your *hair*?'

'Yeah. That.' Suzy held up an acid green strand of hair. 'It was meant to be *A Touch of Mint*, but *somebody* called me this morning when I was dying it and kept me on the phone for ages.'

'Oh no, I'm sorry!' Grace tried to look contrite but couldn't stop the grin spreading across her face.

'Yeah, you look it!' Suzy quipped. 'Anyway, I've got a plan.' She pulled a beanie out of her pocket then shoved it on her head, tucking any stray curls inside. 'What do you think?'

'Well, it definitely covers the green, but won't you be a bit hot?'

Suzy shrugged. 'I'll just sit by a window. And let's face it, it's better than risking Beany seeing it like this. She'd go ballistic!'

When they reached the gate leading on to the pavement, Grace stopped, scanning the road for any sign of the silver car.

'Don't worry, it's gone. I checked as I walked to your house,' Suzy said. 'But I think we should walk to school a different way today, just in case.'

'Good plan. We'll cut through the park. It'll be locked, but I know a way through,' Grace replied.

They walked in silence for a while until they reached

the park.

'I almost forgot, have you heard anything from Georgina May yet?' Suzy asked.

'Not yet. I'm hoping she'll be in touch soon though, so we can find out a bit more,' Grace said as they reached the park. A thick silver chain wound between the gate and the iron railings, keeping the park securely locked up.

'Over here,' she said, gesturing to a section of railing to their right. She pulled at the bottom of one of the rusted metal poles. It swung up and they squeezed through the gap created at the bottom.

'I wonder what she knows?' Suzy mused. 'She must know something for Joan to have said what she did to you. Hey, maybe she knows who the murderer is!'

'I doubt it. If she knew who killed Liv, she'd have gone to the police at the time.'

'Not necessarily. She might have been scared he'd go after her if she told. Or there might not have been any proper proof. Or maybe *she* killed Liv and is deliberately pointing the finger at Johnny. Or–.'

'I get it, I get it!' Grace interrupted her, laughing.

'You can't blame me for getting excited – this is the most exciting thing I've ever been involved in!' Suzy grinned.

When they reached the other end of the park, they could see swathes of students making their way into the school. A large section of the fence in front of them was missing. Yellow tape marked 'KEEP OUT' dangled uselessly from the metal pole to the right of the gap and the pair stepped straight out onto the pavement.

'Hi Grace.' Abeer appeared to Grace's left, falling into step with her. He turned to Suzy. 'Hi, I'm Abeer. I'm in a couple of classes with Grace.'

'Hey. Suzy,' Suzy said with a nod. She looked from Abeer to Grace, and when Abeer turned towards the school building, Suzy raised her eyebrows enquiringly at Grace, a look of approval on her face.

Grace frowned and shook her head, but Suzy ignored her. 'See you at break!' She grinned and hurried ahead, leaving Grace alone with Abeer.

'Isn't your friend hot in that hat?' Abeer asked once

Suzy had gone.

'She doesn't have a choice – she lost a fight with a bottle of green dye.'

'Ah. That explains it. How green is it?'

'Very.'

They pushed their way through the school doors and into the corridor. Abeer stopped at the first door on the left. 'This is me. See you around.' He gave a small salute and disappeared through the door.

Grace hurried on to the next classroom and quickly checked her phone for messages before entering.

Nothing.

She tucked the phone back in the pocket of her backpack and pushed open the door.

It felt like the longest history lesson ever. Grace swore the minute hand hadn't moved at all whenever she checked the time. She was desperate to check her phone for any message from Georgina May, but there was no way she could risk it after the close call in geography the day before.

After what seemed like an eternity, the school bell rang for first break and she sped out of the classroom, pulling her phone out of her pocket.

A missed call message from a number she didn't recognise showed on the home screen.

And they'd left a message! Could it be Georgina May?

Grace hurried along the corridor to the girls' toilets so she could listen to the message there, but when she pushed the door open, there were already three girls in there with their phones out, sharing screens and giggling secretively. She turned back down the corridor and walked out into the playground.

There was a light drizzle, so most of the children sat around the covered picnic benches or were playing on the astro pitch. Grace looked around for somewhere she could take her phone out without being seen by the teachers and was just walking to the back of the sports shed, when Suzy ran up and steered her away.

'Hey, I need to use my phone!' Grace complained.

'Yes. Not there though. Listen.' As if on cue, an unmistakable cackling laugh came from behind the shed. 'Jill Blackburn and her gang are back there,' Suzy explained. 'Tell you what, why don't you stand in the corner of the DT building over there, and I'll stand in front of you with my umbrella so no one can see you. Plus, we'll keep dry,' Suzy suggested. 'Come on.'

Grace followed Suzy to the DT building then stood right in the corner so Suzy could shield her with her umbrella. She looked around to check she was completely hidden. Satisfied, she pulled out her phone and checked her voicemail.

'Hi Grace? It's Georgina May here. Joan Freeman said you wanted to talk to me about my time at Duchesse and ... another matter. If you'd like to meet up, I can meet you in the park after school, maybe by the picnic benches? Just message me with an okay if you can meet and I'll see you there. Bye.'

Grace texted back a quick okay then put her phone away and turned to face Suzy.

'That was Georgina May,' she said. 'She wants to

meet in the park after school.'

'Are you going to meet her?' Suzy asked.

'Yeah, I've got to give it a try. She's the only one who might be able to give us any information about Liv,' Grace replied.

'Do you want me to come with you? It could be dangerous meeting a stranger somewhere that might be a bit secluded. It's one thing meeting in a public café but in a park is completely different.'

'Isn't it your coding club try-out after school today?'

'Yeah, but you're my best friend and I want you to be safe,' Suzy replied.

'Don't worry, Suze, I'll be fine. She's a lady in her 60s after all. Plus, you've been wanting to join coding club since Year 7, so you need to go and blow their socks off. They're going to love your project!' Grace enthused.

'I hope so!'

Just then, the bell rang for end of break, and they made their way back into school.

'Hey, Shrek!' Jill called from behind.

'Ignore them,' Suzy muttered under her breath and

picked up her pace.

'The hat doesn't disguise the fact you've got hair like an ogre!'

Suzy spun round. 'Shrek is bald, you idiot. If you're going to try and insult me, you'll have to do better than that!' she retorted.

They pushed through the doors back into school, leaving Jill Blackburn outside.

'What was that all about?' Grace asked.

Suzy sighed. 'Mr Sedgewick was off sick, so we had a supply teacher. She made me take off my hat in class, so EVERYONE got to see my hair in all its glory, including Jill Blackburn. Just my luck that Sedgewick was off. He wouldn't have minded the beanie. He wears one every day himself.'

'Unlucky,' Grace said. 'How long before it washes out?'

'I dunno. But I'm not waiting. I'm going to buy some black dye after coding try-out.'

Grace stopped outside the French classroom. 'I'll come to yours later to see how you got on and fill you in on what Georgina has to say. Good luck!'

'Thanks, see you later,' Suzy replied, and Grace pushed open the classroom door.

When the bell went for the end of the day, Grace grabbed her things and made her way to the park. The drizzly rain had stopped and the sun was peeking through the clouds, so Grace took her time, enjoying the fresh air after her afternoon of stuffy classrooms. When she reached the picnic benches, she chose one right in the middle so Georgina May would be able to spot her easily. Sitting down, she placed her backpack on the floor between her feet and scanned the park for anyone who might be Georgina. She didn't need to wait long. Within a couple of minutes, a lady approached.

'Hi, are you Grace? I'm Georgina May.' She smiled and her smile lit up her face. Grace instantly warmed to her.

'Yes. Thanks for coming,' she replied, and Georgina

joined her on the picnic bench.

'After what Joan texted me, I was intrigued. She said you were looking into the disappearance of Liv Montague?'

'Um, yes. I spoke to your brother, Frank, on Sunday, but he couldn't really tell me anything. Then I saw Joan and she said you might know a bit more about what happened.'

'You saw Frank? He didn't say anything to me.'

'Oh! Yes, I left him my number to give to you,' Grace said, wondering why Frank hadn't told his sister she'd called round. Maybe Frank did have something to hide after all?

'That's odd,' Georgina said. 'He must have forgotten to give it to me. Not to worry, I'm here now. Anyway, Liv's disappearance. I've got my theories, nothing for certain, of course, but suspicions. Now, before we go into that, just what exactly is your interest in all of this?'

Grace repeated the story she'd told Joan, which seemed to satisfy Georgina too. She nodded.

'So, what would you like to know?'

'Well, I thought it was strange for a young girl to run off to London on her own, so I was wondering if she had a boyfriend?'

'Yes, she did. Oh, she tried to keep it a secret – her parents would never have approved of her having a boyfriend – but everyone knew.'

Grace picked up her bag. 'Would you mind if I make some notes, so I remember what you've said for my project?' she asked.

'Write away.' Georgina paused while Grace took a pad and pen from her backpack and returned the bag to the floor. 'As I was saying, she was seeing a boy called Johnny – Jonathan Bainbridge. All the girls fancied him. He was quite the catch. Not the most handsome boy, but rich and incredibly charismatic. Always surrounded by friends. A bit of a party boy if you know what I mean.'

'How did Liv meet him? Duchesse was an all-girls school, wasn't it?'

'Yes, but that didn't stop Liv. Johnny was a senior at St Martin's – the local private boys' school – and they met at a formal dance held for the seniors of Duchesse and St Martin's. Liv was there to serve the fruit punch. She was too young to attend, but she was so beautiful and so … spirited … Johnny asked her to dance and the rest, as they say, is history.'

'Do you know if Johnny still lives around here? I'd love to be able to talk to him too,' Grace asked.

Georgina's face darkened. 'No. He moved away after Liv disappeared. The whole family did. His father owned a big multinational company, so they didn't have any real ties to Chesterford apart from it being where his grandfather had set up the company originally. I don't know where he went and didn't care to find out.'

'It doesn't sound as though you liked him much?'

'No. Well, between you and me, he may have been popular and rich, but he had a mean streak. I can't count the number of times Liv came to me in tears because he'd said something nasty. Anyone who could treat Liv like that wasn't worth worrying about.' She looked at her watch. 'I'm afraid I'm going to have to go in a minute,' she said apologetically.

'Could I ask one last question?' Grace asked.

Georgina nodded.

'Do you think Liv ran away to London to become a model?'

'No. No, I don't. I didn't at the time, and I still don't think she'd have done that without telling me first. We told each other everything, and she'd have been far too excited to keep something like that to herself. No. Something happened to Liv. I'm sure of it. I just don't know what.'

She stood and Grace followed suit.

'Thanks so much, Miss May. You've given me lots to work on.'

'Well, if you do find out what happened to Liv, I'd love to hear about it.'

'Absolutely. And if you think of anything else, could you pop me a text?' Grace asked as she picked up her bag and put the pad and pen inside.

'Of course. I've got your number.'

Georgina turned to leave before turning back, a look

of concern on her face. 'If you're planning on looking into Johnny, please be careful.'

'What do you mean?'

'Johnny's from a prominent family and I'm sure, wherever he is, he won't want any mud to be flung his way. In fact, I'm sure he would do anything to stop it.' Georgina turned then and walked away, leaving Grace frozen to the spot.

He'd do anything? Did that include having her followed?

CHAPTER 17

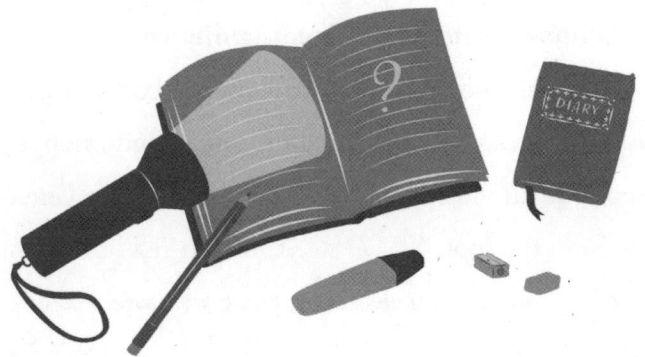

Grace walked to Suzy's house in a daze, a thousand thoughts whizzing around her head. Had her visions been real? Did Johnny Bainbridge really kill Liv? What did Frank May have to do with any of it? As she walked up the driveway in front of Suzy's house, Grace took out her phone to send the usual text, but before she could type anything, the door was wrenched open by an out-of-breath Suzy.

'I saw you walk up the path,' she panted, pushing

her glasses back up on her nose. 'Come up.'

Grace followed her friend up the stairs.

'Hey, how did the try-out for coding club go?' she asked as they took the second flight of stairs.

'Great! I think I'm in. They loved my project, but they've got other people to see, so I won't hear for a week or so.' Suzy grinned, holding up her hand with her fingers crossed.

'Brilliant. Well done you! I knew you'd blow them away.'

When they got to the attic room, Suzy flopped onto a white swivel chair at her desk and wiggled her mouse. The monitor sprang to life and was filled with diagrams and text.

Grace moved directly behind her to see more clearly. On the screen was a plan of what they'd found out so far with lines linking people and places together.

'You've been busy!' she said.

'Yeah, well I've seen your note-taking *and* your handwriting, so I thought we should get everything down so we can actually *read it*!' Suzy joked. 'I've also logged who you've spoken to, what the outcome was and who you've still got to speak to.' With a click of her mouse, the screen changed to a spreadsheet of names, dates and notes.

'Well, it's definitely organised! And,' Grace added, pulling out her notebook, 'I've got more from Georgina May!' Suzy looked over, squinting to make out Grace's scrawl and failing miserably.

'You're going to have to tell me – I've got no idea what any of that says!'

Grace filled her in on her conversation earlier.

'So, it looks like the Johnny from your vision was this Jonathan Bainbridge. It'd explain why he disappeared straight after Liv did. I bet his family found out he killed her and sent him away,' Suzy said when Grace had finished.

'Don't get carried away! Let's research him and see what we can find out.'

Suzy minimised the list of names and opened a new search. 'How's his name spelt?' she asked, her fingers hovering over the keyboard.

'J-O-N-A-T-H-A-N B-A-I-N-B-R-I-D-G-E.'

Suzy's fingers raced across the keys. 'Right, let's see what we've got.' A list of Jonathan Bainbridges flashed up on the screen. 'We're going to have to narrow it down a bit. What else do you know about him?'

Grace read over her notes. 'Nothing about Johnny directly, but I do know his dad owned a big company that was owned by his dad before him. He set it up in Chesterford.'

Suzy deleted the search and entered Bainbridge Chesterford. A new list of websites appeared. 'Bingo!' She clicked on the first link. Chesterford Town's own web page appeared, displaying an article about the history of the town's clock tower. It had been donated and built by Albert Bainbridge in 1901, father of Thomas Bainbridge who'd continued his father's manufacturing business.

She returned to the search results and took another look at the list of sites.

'How about that one?' Grace said, pointing to a link about halfway down the page.

Suzy clicked on it. It was the website for Bainbridge Automation and Robotics. She clicked on the *About* tab and scrolled through the information about the history of the company and its visions for the future.

She stopped.

There, at the bottom, was a link to a video, showing a picture of a smiling man in his 60s. His black hair was still thick but greying at the temples.

Grace pressed *Play*.

On screen, Jonathan Bainbridge spoke about the company's history and how it had evolved since he took it over from his father and then his visions for the future. He was well spoken with a rich, deep voice that had an almost hypnotic quality to it. Even after all these years, Grace could immediately see what Liv had seen in Johnny.

His eyes though, which were the palest grey she had ever seen, had a coldness about them that chilled her, even through the screen.

'That's him!' Suzy shouted.

'So, he runs the business now. Let's see if we can

find out anything else about him.'

Suzy clicked on the *Contact Us* tab and located the head office – London. That's where Johnny would be now.

'Okay, so we know who Johnny is and where he is. What do we do now? We can't tie the murder to him, but we can't just let him get away with it!' Grace exclaimed.

'I know, but there's not much we can do. It's not like we can go to see him in London and confront him. If he really did kill Liv, there's no way he'd confess it to us. Plus, he probably wouldn't think twice about silencing two meddling teenagers if it meant he wouldn't be exposed as a murderer.' Suzy raked her hand through her hair and sighed. 'I can't believe I'm going to my cousin's wedding this weekend. Just when we've got a lead! AND Mum says it's unlikely there'll be any internet where we're going!'

'I know, but he killed her over 50 years ago – another few days won't harm. Just go and enjoy yourself.'

'You're right. But of all the times!' Suzy frowned.

'Your mum's away this weekend too, isn't she? Didn't you say she had a conference or something? Will you be okay on your own?'

'Yeah, but she's only away Saturday night and I'll be staying with Annie over the road, so I'll be fine,' Grace reassured her. 'Plus, you'll be back on Sunday morning.'

'Okay, as long as you're sure. I'll send you the notes I've made, so if you want to have a look at them while I'm gone, then you can.' Suzy unplugged her laptop, closed it and placed it inside a white case. 'I'll take this with me too, just in case.'

'Thanks, Suze. Have a brilliant time and don't worry about me.' She hugged her friend and left with a wave over her shoulder.

As she walked round the corner to her own street, her heartbeat quickened until she'd checked every single car to make sure the silver car from earlier wasn't there. Then she smiled to herself. He *had* just been a weirdo after all.

CHAPTER 18

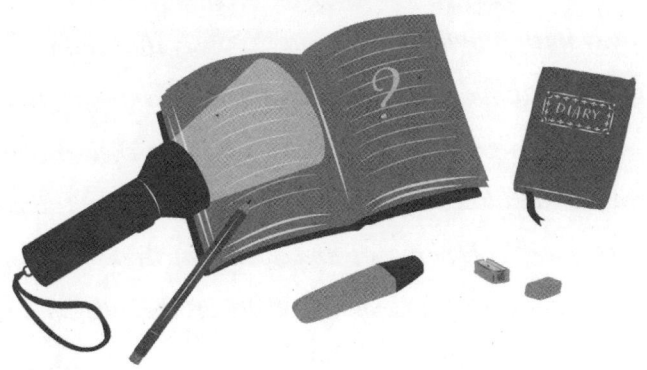

'*Yes?*' Frank answered.

'*I've got news. I installed spyware on both of the girls' computers while they were at school, and they're both on Suzy's now looking up a Jonathan Bainbridge. They seemed pretty determined but stopped when they found the company he works for and where it's based.*'

'Blast!' Frank spat. They'd found out far more than he'd ever expected.

'*Don't worry, I've got access to the microphones on their*

phones and laptops, so I can listen too, and they've got no idea what to do with the information they've found. Plus, the girl is home alone most of this weekend – her friend's away until Sunday and her mum's away this weekend – so I don't think they'll be doing any research for a while.'

Frank digested this information. 'Keep checking the searches and listen in – you can do that remotely. I'll sort out Grace Yi.' He hung up and called a different number.

'You've got good news?' the voice on the other end of the line said without preamble.

'Not exactly,' Frank admitted. 'It seems the girls know who you are.'

There was silence on the line. Then, 'I want you to take things further. Do whatever it takes to stop them finding out more. And I mean whatever it takes. Do you understand? And Frank?'

'Yes?'

'I'm relying on you. Don't let me down.'

The other man hung up and Frank stared at the phone in his hand. Things had gone much further than he'd anticipated.

CHAPTER 19

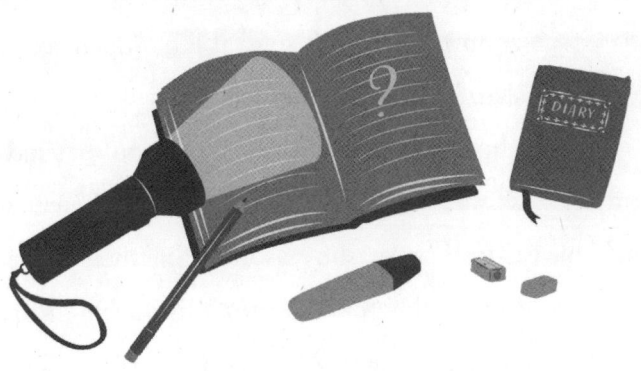

The next few days of school dragged. On the plus side, Grace had plenty of time to think about what the next step in the investigation should be, and when her alarm went off at 9am on Saturday morning, she was more than ready for a bit of action. She sat up in bed and grabbed her laptop. A few clicks later, a satellite map of the area was on the screen.

'Right …' she said to herself. 'Let's see if I can find out where you were killed.'

The image was of the area directly around Liv's house, Barrington Grange. There were no areas of open grassland on the map like she'd seen in her visions, so Grace zoomed out until several large open spaces were revealed.

Grace thought for a moment. Liv wouldn't have travelled too far on a date. Plus, Johnny had a car so he'd have driven closer, she reasoned. She then worked through each of the possible sites, eliminating those that were too far away to be likely. This left seven possibilities. But how to tell which of them was the site from her visions?

She zoomed in as close as possible on each of them, but they still looked identical. She needed to think of something else.

Grace turned the laptop off and went downstairs.

'Do you want some toast?' she shouted to her mum.

'Love some.'

Grace went into the kitchen, put the bread in the toaster and poured a cup of coffee from the pot on the counter. Then she went to the fridge and removed some butter, milk and juice for herself and placed them on the counter too. The toast popped and she pulled it from the toaster, dropping it onto a plate and blowing on her fingers. As she spread the butter, a thought struck her.

The diary!

She quickly splashed milk into the coffee and took the mug and the toast through to her mum. Then she raced upstairs and grabbed the diary from her bedside table. She flicked to the final entry. It was from the day that Liv disappeared.

8.8 JB 1:00 GM

JB must be Johnny, but where was GM?

She checked the map again. One location jumped off the screen.

Grant's Meadow.

That was where Liv met Johnny.

Where Liv was murdered.

She was certain of it.

Grace shoved her phone in her bag and ran back to the kitchen, taking two large bites of each piece of toast and gulping down her juice before returning to her mum's office.

'Just going out for a bit, I'll be back for lunch.'

'Well, enjoy yourself,' her mum said, taking a sip of the coffee before looking back at the paperwork on her desk.

Grace turned to leave.

'Oh, Grace? Have you remembered I'm away at the conference tonight?' she asked.

'Yeah. What time are you going?' Grace asked.

'I should be done here by about 11, so I'll head off then. If you're not back by the time I leave, I'll put a pie in the fridge, so you'll just need to heat it up for tea. Oh, and Annie's left a key for you. She's got her book club ladies over tonight, so she said you can let yourself in,' she added, passing Grace a front door key.

'Thanks, Mum,' Grace said, attaching the key to her keyring.

'And Grace? Please take care while I'm gone. I know you said that you've not seen that car since I spoke to the driver, but I want you to promise me you'll lock all of the doors when you're in the house by yourself. And that you'll be home before dark. And that you'll phone me if you're worried about anything. Anything at all.'

Grace smiled. 'I promise. You don't need to worry about me, just go and get that promotion. You deserve it.'

'Okay then, see you later,' her mum said.

Grace waved and hurried out of the front door.

CHAPTER 20

On the other side of town, Frank May's phone rang.

'Yes?'

'She's getting close. She's been checking maps of the area and zoomed in on the place you told me about. But she's also been looking at a few other places.'

Frank was silent while he absorbed the news. How did the girl know to look at grasslands? He shook his head.

'Okay. Keep watching for now and don't let her out of your sight. I need to know exactly where she goes.'

'No problem. If she does decide to visit the sites though, I won't be able to follow her. She'd spot me in a heartbeat out in the open.'

'I don't care!' Frank snapped. 'Just sort it!'

The line was silent for a moment.

'Alright. I've got a plan. Leave it to me,' the man replied.

'Good. I'll be in touch.'

Frank hung up and raked his fingers through his hair. What a mess ...

CHAPTER 21

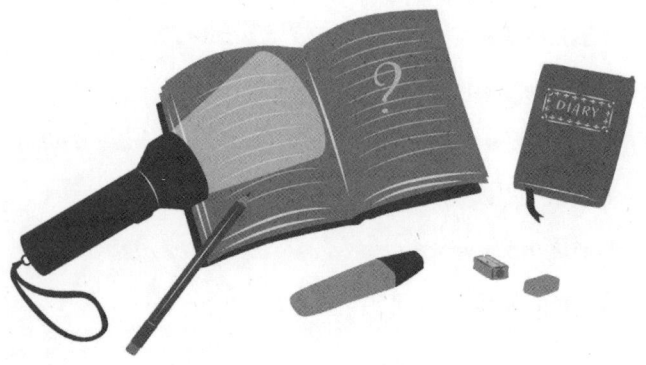

The sun was bright, just as it had been on the day Liv was murdered, and the similarity made Grace quicken her pace. She was certain she was going to find *something* today – she could just feel it. Laughter and noisy chatter flowed from the back gardens of the row of terraced houses on her left, and she smiled as she dodged a girl whizzing along the pavement on her scooter. The hedges were alive with birds, and their songs filled the air as they darted in and out of the branches. A small white dog pushed its nose through a gate as she passed, and she bent to stroke its head and give it a scratch behind the ears.

'Hey there,' she said, smiling as it yapped and ran in circles, its tail wagging furiously. She straightened up and looked around.

Ahead of her, Grace could just make out the spire of St Peter's church – the first landmark on her journey to the potential murder site. The narrow road was free of cars and a group of boys and girls had set up a makeshift football pitch on it. The corners and goalposts were marked out with jumpers and coats. As she walked past, the ball trickled over to her and she nudged it back with her foot.

'Thanks!' one of the boys yelled. 'Our throw in!'

'No! Your team kicked it out!'

'Did not! It bounced off Blane's leg!'

'No, it …'

'Car!' one of the girls shouted as Grace passed her, and the other children hurried to clear the road. Grace turned.

A short way behind her, a black car had stopped, waiting for the road to clear before it could continue. In no time, the goalposts had been moved and the car continued on its way. Grace glanced through the passenger window as it glided past, its engine a low purr. A young man was driving, his eyes covered by large sunglasses. He briefly glanced at Grace as he passed, and then the car disappeared around the corner.

Grace continued on her journey, and in no time, she arrived at the church. Its sandstone walls glowed orange in the sunlight, and the stained-glass windows shone as though illuminated from inside. Grace opened the black wrought iron gate and followed a cobbled path which ran along the left side of the church towards the cemetery at the rear. As she walked between the gravestones, Grace marvelled at the ornate carvings and statues that adorned some of the graves: a cherub playing a lyre, a beautiful angel with outstretched wings, a praying Madonna.

Grace glanced at the inscriptions that were etched

into the stones and her thoughts once again turned to Liv. Would *she* ever get to have a burial plot? To have somewhere to rest in peace? Or would she forever remain in an unmarked grave somewhere?

It occurred to Grace then, that finding Liv was the most important thing – not finding her killer. Liv needed her. She needed to be brought home to rest.

Grace was just wondering what kind of stone would be placed on Liv's grave, when a figure ran out from behind one of the gravestones and she was knocked to the ground. Her bag flew off her shoulder, spewing its contents all over the path.

'Oh, I am so sorry!' A man stepped over to her as Grace clambered back to her feet. 'Here, let me get that for you.' He bent down to pick the spilled items up off the ground and started to put them back in the bag.

'Here, I'll do that. Don't worry,' Grace said, holding her hand out for her bag.

The man stood up and Grace recognised him immediately. It was the man from the black car. He was taller than Grace had thought from seeing him in the car, and he was wearing a close-fitting black t-shirt, black jeans and black trainers. His bare arms were tanned and toned and a tattoo of a serpent snaked up his left bicep before disappearing under the sleeve of his t-shirt. Although he was still wearing his sunglasses, Grace could tell that he kept glancing over her shoulder to the church behind her.

'Um. Will you be okay? I'm afraid I need to hurry off – I've got an appointment with the vicar and I'm running late already. I was so busy looking at my watch that I didn't even see you until it was too late!'

Grace smiled. 'I'm fine, really. You don't need to stay. I wouldn't want to make you late for the vicar!'

'Thanks!' the man replied. He hurried along the side of the church before turning the corner at the front. Grace finished packing her bag, slung it back onto her shoulder, and continued through the graveyard.

CHAPTER 22

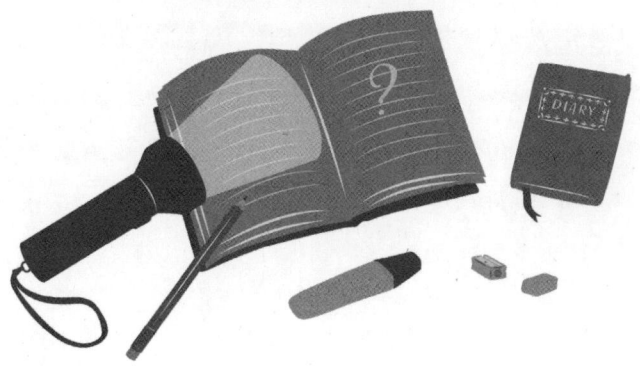

Once around the front of the church, the man stepped deep into the shadows of the entrance vestibule and waited. All was quiet, except for the passing of an occasional car and melodic twitter of birdsong in the trees.

After several minutes, when he was sure Grace had moved on, the man emerged out into the sunshine and glanced around the back of the church. The girl was nowhere to be seen. Silently, he jogged towards his car parked directly outside, opened the door and climbed *inside. Then he removed two objects from his pocket and placed them on the passenger seat beside him.*

Grace's phone.

And her house keys.

He turned the key in the ignition and the engine rumbled to life.

Time to put the second part of his plan into action.

CHAPTER 23

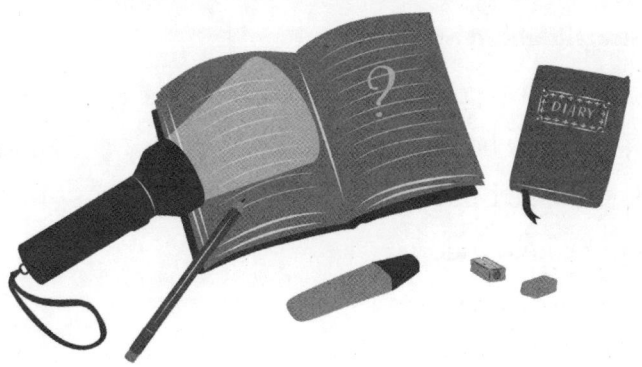

Grace, meanwhile, had made her way through the cemetery and out of the gate at the rear of the church grounds. There, she found herself on a wide road lined with trees adorned with leaves of every shade of red, orange and gold imaginable. They glowed in the sunlight with the brilliance of a bonfire and Grace was transfixed. Either side, set well back from the road, stood magnificent detached houses, each one different to the last. Grace's fingers itched to sketch them –

the twisting chimney stacks, the climbing roses, the turrets and the ornate roof lines. But she refused to be distracted, keeping her eyes fixed on the pavement straight ahead of her.

The further away from the church she walked, the sparser the houses became, until the very last house had slipped out of view and she found herself in open countryside.

Grace stopped.

The site was vast.

How would she ever find where Liv met Johnny? She pulled her notepad from her bag and flipped the pages until she found what she needed – the sketch of her vision of the murder. She glanced at the drawing, then at the landscape around her, repeating the process until she had turned a full circle. It all looked so very different from her picture. Was she in the wrong place or was it different because so many years had passed? Even if she *was* in the right place, would it look anything like the one in her drawing? Grace sighed and studied her picture more closely but nothing helped.

Grace put the notebook back in her bag and retraced her steps back home.

When she reached her house, she groped around in her bag for her house keys. Unable to find them straight away, she knelt and emptied the bag's contents onto the path.

No keys.

She closed her eyes and groaned. They must have fallen out at the cemetery and not been picked up with the rest of her stuff. She quickly put everything back in her bag and rang the doorbell.

'One second!' Her mum's muffled voice came from inside. Moments later she pulled open the front door. 'Grace? Did you leave your keys? It's a good job I'm a bit late leaving!' She gestured to her overnight case in the hallway. 'Do *not* leave your keys while I'm gone. But if you do, Annie's got a spare. Anyway, as I said, I'm late. Take care. Call me if you need anything. Love you. Make sure you lock the door behind me!' She picked up her case, kissing Grace on the cheek and giving her a hug as she left the house.

'Bye, Mum!' Grace called after her mum's retreating figure. She closed the front door and ran upstairs, flinging her bag and coat on the bed before going into the bathroom. Then, she returned to her bedroom and reached for her bag.

Grace frowned.

There, on top of the bedside table, were her phone and keys. Confused, she picked them up. She could have sworn she'd packed them in her bag. Shaking her head, she put her phone in her pocket and placed the keys back on the bedside table. As she did, she spotted a faint mark on her cream carpet. She knelt down to take a closer look.

It was a footprint.

A man's footprint.

Ashen faced, Grace scanned the rest of the floor. Although they were faint, she could clearly make out a trail of footprints from her bedroom door to her bed, before they faded and disappeared completely. Someone had been in her house. In her *room*. Then, a single terrifying thought occurred to her.

What if they were still here?

Grace pulled out her phone and called Suzy, holding her breath as she waited for it to dial through. 'Hi, this is Suzy …' came the voicemail message.

She hung up and called her mum instead. This time it did ring out, but no answer. Grace mentally kicked herself. Her mum would be driving and always left her phone on the back seat so she wouldn't be tempted to answer it. *What now?* She could send her mum a text message, but by the time she'd driven to Edinburgh and read it, there wouldn't be any point. Besides, it would distract her from the conference, and Grace knew how important it was. She couldn't disturb her for a footprint.

Grace stood up and paced the floor. She'd have to check the house herself. She picked up the glass bottle filled with solar fairy lights that she kept on her bedside table and held it upside down by its neck. Not the best weapon, but it would have to do. Then she looked around her room. Where could somebody hide?

The wardrobe.

With her heart pounding in her ears, Grace tiptoed silently across the room and reached for the handle. *One. Two. Three.* Grace yanked open the door, leaping back onto her bed as it flew open.

The wardrobe was empty.

From her position on the bed, Grace checked the room for any other possible hiding places. Her heart froze in her chest. There *was* one other hiding place.

Under the bed.

The bed she was standing on.

The bed that she'd have to step off to get down to the floor.

Why didn't I check there first? she chastised herself, her mind filling with images of scary films she'd seen where the bad guys almost always hid under the bed. There was only one thing for it. Grace took a deep breath and leapt over to the doorway. As soon as her feet hit the floor, she spun around and crouched to look under the bed.

Clear.

One room down.

With her heart now pounding against her ribs, Grace edged out onto the landing and checked her mum's bedroom and bathroom. Both were empty. She tiptoed down the stairs, being careful not to tread on the squeaky steps and checked the downstairs rooms.

All were empty.

With a sigh of relief, Grace placed the bottle on the kitchen worktop and sank into a stool at the island. She was alone, but whose footprints were they? Grace was certain they hadn't been there that morning, so somebody must have been in her room while she was out. But then her mum had been in. Surely she'd have had to have let them in? A thought occurred to Grace then. The roofer. Her mum must have had the roofer over to check the small leak she'd had during the heavy rain the previous month. That must be it. Grace resolved to ask her mum when she next spoke to her and glanced at her watch. 2pm. Only another twenty hours before Suzy was due back. She drummed her fingers on the kitchen counter. What to do now?

Grace stepped off the stool and checked the back

door was locked, then went to the front door and checked that too.

Happy the house was secure, she walked through to the living room and flopped onto the cream leather sofa before grabbing the TV remote control. She flicked distractedly through the channels, but she didn't really see the pictures on the screen. Her mind was somewhere else entirely. After she'd flicked through all the channels twice, she flung the remote onto the seat next to her and climbed the stairs to her bedroom. She *had* to do something.

Grace opened her laptop and brought up the map of Grant's Meadow, hoping for a clue. Anything to show where Liv might have met Johnny. But there was nothing.

What now?

Grace thought for a moment.

Maybe there's something in the diary I've missed. Now I know GM is Grant's Meadow perhaps some of the other notes will make sense? She picked up the diary and copied down all the references to GM. There were twenty altogether, but one had another pair of letters.

13.3 JB 10:00 GM CC

She returned to the map, scouring the screen, but her hope dissolved to dust. Nowhere had the initials CC.

She opened her search engine instead and typed in Places in Chesterfield CC.

A list of entries appeared on screen, all about Chesterfield Cricket Club.

She tapped her finger on the keyboard, thinking what else she could check. She thought back to her geography lessons when they'd covered map skills and then it hit her. Last year, her class had entered a national orienteering competition, in which they'd had to use Ordnance Survey maps. She remembered the instructor explaining that Ordnance Survey maps showed lots more information than a regular map.

Quickly, she brought up a map of the local area and zoomed in on Grant's Meadow. She saw the location straight away.

Cooper's Cross.

It was right in the middle of Grant's Meadow and

wouldn't have been visible from any road or public footpath. The perfect place to meet a boyfriend in secret.

And the perfect place to commit a murder.

She looked at her watch. She should have time to get there and have a look around before it started to get dark. Before any doubts could seep into her mind, Grace grabbed her bag, stashed the phone and keys inside and left the house.

The journey back to Grant's Meadow was uneventful, but this time, she followed the map to Cooper's Cross at its centre. Once there, she pulled her sketchbook out of her backpack and looked around.

It was a perfect match.

She was in the right place!

But she still didn't know the exact spot Liv was murdered, and without that, they'd never convince the police that Johnny killed her. She scanned the area, looking for a clue. Any clue.

Then, a flash of colour caught her eye.

Grace walked towards it and there, conspicuous amongst the rough grass and gnarly bushes, was a rose bush covered in tiny pink buds.

Grace looked around. There were no other roses as far as she could see. Maybe … just maybe … She checked her drawing one more time. It was an almost perfect match, from the hill in the background to the oak tree to her right – only a young tree in her vision but now tall with sprawling branches. Johnny must have planted the rose bush. Perhaps he'd felt guilty for what he had done?

Grace grabbed her phone and tried Suzy, but it went straight to voicemail *again*.

She considered her next step. She could come back tomorrow with Suzy, and they could dig around and see what they could find. After all, there wasn't anything she could do there now. Her mind made up, Grace took a photo of the rose bush to show Suzy. Then she turned to leave.

She'd only taken a few steps when an idea struck her. She quickly checked the front pocket of her bag for the remaining money from when she'd bought her coat. It was still there. Then, she searched Hardware Stores near me, and a list popped up on the screen along with a map. She selected the first on the list – Frampton's Home and Garden – and a map appeared. It was just off the main road she'd walked on to get here. Happy she knew where she was going, Grace packed everything away and made her way there.

The shop was small and its bay window was filled with all sorts of items for the home, from whisks and bins to coat hangers and party balloons. Grace paused at the door, tendrils of doubt creeping into her mind. *Maybe I should call the police? No. If there's nothing there and I've wasted their time, they'll be angry and will probably call my mum and she'll be angry I left the house. Maybe I should wait for Suzy?* Grace dismissed that thought straight away. If they did actually find anything, she'd only throw up on the evidence, just like she had with the rabbit.

She was on her own.

I can do this.

Grace pushed any doubts from her mind as she pushed open the door. The inside of the shop was much the same as the outside but was split into small sections. Grace walked past kitchen goods and pet supplies before arriving at the area she wanted.

Gardening equipment.

And there, right in the middle of the section, was a fork, a spade and a rake. Grace checked the price of the spade. £20.99. She only had £15.

'Can I help you?' came a voice from behind, startling her. Grace turned round to see an elderly gentleman. His head was bald apart from two white tufts above his ears, and a pair of wire-rimmed glasses was perched on his nose.

'After a spade, are you?'

'Um, yes,' Grace replied. 'But I was hoping to find something cheaper.'

'Ah, you'll want the discontinued section. Follow me,' the man said, hobbling towards the back of the shop. They arrived in front of a garden wheelie bin filled with a variety of bits and bobs. 'I'm sure there was one in here the other day,' the man said, reaching in. 'Hang on a tick.'

Grace watched as he seemed to pull out anything with a handle – a rake, a weed remover, just a handle with nothing on the end of it – until, with a victorious 'Aha!' he pulled out a shovel. It was a bit scratched and a bit bent but was just what she needed. 'How's this then?' He peered at the price tag. 'This one's £12.50, down from £25.'

Grace grinned. 'That's great! I'll take it!'

The old man slowly walked to the till just in front of the window. 'Doing a bit of gardening, are you?' he asked as he put in the amount and tied a bag around the handle to show she'd paid.

'Something like that,' Grace replied with a smile then left the shop and made her way back to the rose bush with a determined spring in her step.

When she got there, she looked around to check she was still alone – she didn't want anyone asking questions about why she was digging. With no one in sight, she pushed the blade of the spade into the ground and began to dig.

CHAPTER 24

Frank's phone vibrated in his pocket. He quickly glanced at the screen.

'Excuse me, just got to take this. Back in a jiffy!' He stood up from the dining table, smiling an apology at his sister and their guests.

'What is it?' he hissed as he closed the door to the hallway behind him.

'It's me. Bad news. I added some spyware to the girl's phone so I can access her GPS–'

'And?' Frank interrupted.

'And, she's found the location.'

Silence rang from the phone.

'Boss? Are you there?'

'What …? Yes, I'm still here,' Frank replied. *'You're sure she's found it?'*

'Positive.'

Frank cursed.

'It's time to finish the job. You need to silence her. Now. She can't let anyone know what she's found. Ever.'

'Not me, Frank. I just agreed to watch her. Killing kids was never part of my contract with Mr Bainbridge. You'll have to find someone else for that.'

'I'll pay you extra,' Frank offered.

'No chance. You're on your own,' the watcher said and hung up.

Frank paced the length of the hallway, bracing himself for the call he had to make next. Johnny would not be happy. Worse still, he knew exactly how Grace had found the site of Liv's murder. Why, oh why, had he planted that wretched rose bush?

The phone rang once before it was picked up.

'Are you calling to tell me you've sorted the girl, Frank?' Johnny answered.

'There's been a problem, Johnny. The girl's found Liv's grave.'

The line was silent.

'Johnny? Did you hear what I said?' Frank asked.

'I heard, Frank. But I was waiting for me to tell me it was a joke. It is a joke, isn't it, Frank?'

'Um …'

Johnny let out an exaggerated sigh.

'I didn't want it to come to this, after all, you've always been loyal. But mess this up and the original of the photo I sent you will be posted to the police. And you know what that means, don't you?'

Johnny hung up.

With trembling fingers, Frank replaced the phone in his pocket then stepped into the downstairs toilet. His ashen face stared back at him from the mirror above the sink. How was he going to get out of this mess? He turned on the tap and splashed his face with cold water before looking in the mirror again and fixing a smile on his face. Not wholly convincing, but it'd have to do. He had a dinner party to get back to.

Frank walked back through to the dining room and Georgina looked up as he entered. 'Come on, Frank, you can't miss blowing out the candles on your own birthday cake!' she said. As if on cue, the door to the kitchen swung open revealing a large rectangular birthday cake covered in lit candles.

Grace Yi would have to wait.

CHAPTER 25

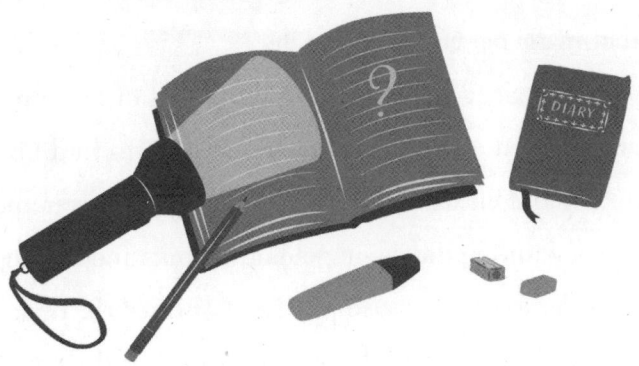

It felt like she'd been digging for hours, but the hole in front of Grace didn't seem like it was getting bigger. Putting down the spade, she straightened her complaining back and wiped at the sweat on her brow with her sleeve.

The sun was already starting its descent, and she knew she'd only have a couple more hours of daylight left. She had to keep going. Grace pulled her sleeves over her sore hands, picked up the spade once again and thrust it into the ground. Luckily, the soil hadn't turned to clay as she dug deeper and her spade cut through easily. It was hauling the earth out of the hole that made her entire body ache.

She pushed her aches and pains out of her mind and focused on why she was doing this – to find Liv.

On and on she dug, and the sun slipped lower and lower, painting the sky in golds and pinks and making it harder to see. Grace stopped and assessed the trench that she'd dug around the rose bush. She'd been so confident that the rose bush must have been planted by Johnny at the site he'd buried Liv, but maybe she'd been wrong. Her hole had made an almost complete ring around the bush, and she'd found absolutely nothing except for several old cans, a one-pound coin and a bent coat hanger. Still, there was only about a metre left to dig.

She couldn't give up now.

Grace began to dig once more, first taking out the layer of grass, then cutting into the dark, peaty soil below. 20cm down. Nothing. 40cm. Nothing. She'd dug nearly half a metre down all the way around the bush. Surely Johnny wouldn't have dug down more than that to bury Liv? After all, he'd have wanted to get rid of the body as quickly as possible, and he could hardly have left her body lying on the grass for hours while he dug the grave.

Grace plunged her spade into the earth with renewed determination. Vibrations jarred through her hand and up her arm as it struck something solid. She knelt down and used the blade of the spade to scrape away the soil, careful not to damage whatever it was she'd hit. The dying sun glinted off something smooth. Grace's heart sank. *Another* bit of rubbish.

She pushed her spade under the object and levered it up. Once it was free of the ground, she dropped the shovel and fell to her knees to get a better look.

In front of her was a broken cola bottle *exactly* like the one she'd seen in her visions.

The label had completed rotted away, but it was the same shape and its bottom had broken off. Grace wiped away more dirt to get a closer look but then stopped.

Would there be DNA on the bottle? She'd seen plenty of detective dramas where cold cases were solved by matching the DNA of the killer from years ago using new evidence or new lab techniques that weren't around at the time of the murder. But would Liv or Johnny's DNA still be on the bottle after all this time buried in the ground? Grace didn't want to risk destroying evidence.

She climbed out of the hole to grab the plastic bag the owner of the hardware store had wrapped around the handle of the spade. Then she carefully scooped the bottle up into it, avoiding the jagged edges of the broken glass, which still looked dangerously sharp after all this time.

Grace no longer noticed her aches and pains – she'd found it! She'd found where Liv had been murdered!

She sank onto her hands and knees again, ignoring the spade, and pulled the soil aside with her hands. Dirt clogged under her fingernails and small pieces of stone scraped against her skin, but Grace barely noticed. In no time, her fingers brushed against another hard object. Carefully, she rubbed away the soil with her fingertips, and inch by inch it was slowly revealed to her. The item was long and thin, but so dirty she couldn't immediately make out what it was in the fading light. Grace stood up, climbed out of the hole and walked over to her bag. She pulled out her phone and returned to the hole. She stepped down and propped it next to the object. Then she turned on the torch and started cleaning it more thoroughly.

Until she saw exactly what it was.

A bone.

Grace sat back on her haunches, disbelief, sadness and joy flooding through her.

She'd done it.

She'd found Liv.

Grace carefully placed the bone in the plastic bag with the broken bottle and tightly tied the handles together before stepping out of the hole. She looked at the ditch she had dug. The rest of Liv's body would be buried in the earth too, but she didn't have the strength to dig any more.

Grace picked up her phone and dialled the number for the local police station, but before the call could even ring out, she hung up. Would they bother coming out for a teenager saying they'd found a bone? Unless they saw it in person, they'd be bound to think it was just an animal bone. She *could* go straight to the police station and show them, but she'd rather do that with Suzy at her side for support.

Deciding that she'd go to the police station in the morning, Grace glanced at the ditch once more and her shoulders sagged as she realised she'd have to fill it in. She couldn't leave the grave exposed to scavenging wildlife. Grace picked up her spade, scraped the soil back into the hole then stamped it down to make the area less conspicuous if anyone did happen to walk this way. When she'd finished, she looked it over. Not bad. If anyone did come along, they *could* just think that someone had been gardening around the rose bush. Satisfied, she picked up the plastic bag and spade, and started the long journey home.

When she finally arrived, Grace leant the spade

against the side of her house then crossed the road to Annie's. As soon as she opened the front door, she was greeted by the sounds of chatter and laughter. The book club was clearly still in full swing. Grace reached for the handle to the living room but immediately spotted how filthy her hands were. Suspecting her face wouldn't be much better, she stepped into the downstairs toilet to wash before entering the living room.

'Oh, hi love,' Annie said, smiling up at Grace from the sofa. 'You're in the front spare bedroom like last time. Help yourself to anything you need. I'll be leaving at about 6am tomorrow, so just lock up when you're ready. I'll pick the key up from your mum tomorrow.'

Grace thanked her and made her way upstairs. Once in her bedroom, she flung her backpack on the floor at the end of her bed then carefully placed the plastic bag on top of the chest of drawers.

Next she grabbed her phone and tried Suzy one more time. The phone went to voicemail again, and Grace tossed her phone onto the bedside table. Using the very last traces of energy, Grace flopped back on her bed. Exhaustion immediately took over, and she was asleep as soon as her head hit the pillow.

When the alarm woke Grace at 9am, she was momentarily surprised to find herself fully dressed. Then, the events of yesterday flooded back to her. She leapt out of bed and moaned as every muscle in her body complained.

Slowly, she hobbled back home and climbed straight into the shower. The hot water pummelled her aching muscles and she sighed. With her mum away, Grace took the opportunity to have a *really* long shower, and when she emerged after thirty minutes, she felt revitalised. After drying her hair and pulling on some leggings and a t-shirt, Grace checked the time.

Suzy would be home soon.

Smiling, she went downstairs, grabbed some toast and orange juice then took them upstairs. She sat on her bed and placed the plate of toast and juice on her bedside table. Suzy wasn't going to believe what had happened in the last twenty-four hours! At 10 o'clock exactly, Grace picked up her phone and called.

Suzy picked up on the first ring.

'You won't believe how terrible my weekend's been,' Suzy started, without even saying hello. 'I never thought I'd say it, but school will be awesome in comparison.'

Grace smiled. 'Oh Suzy, it can't have been all that bad, can it?'

'You think? I was sat between Great Aunt Mabel, who's as deaf as a post, so I had to say everything about twenty times and Cousin Harriet, who had her baby with her. The little monster kept smearing his food all over the table and doing the stinkiest poos ever. It was awful. And I mean AWFUL,' Suzy sighed dramatically.

'Well, you'll never guess what happened here yesterday,' Grace began, but Suzy interrupted.

'Grace? Is your mum home?'

'No, she's away until tonight. But Suze, listen. I found—'

'Grace. Listen to me.' The urgency in Suzy's voice stopped Grace in her tracks.

'What?'

'You're absolutely sure your mum's not home?'

'Yes, Suze, wh–'

'There's someone in your house. Grace. I'm looking out of my window, and there's someone in your kitchen!'

Icy fear slithered down Grace's spine.

'Grace, I can't see them any more. They've left the kitchen. You need to get out of there. Right now!'

CHAPTER 26

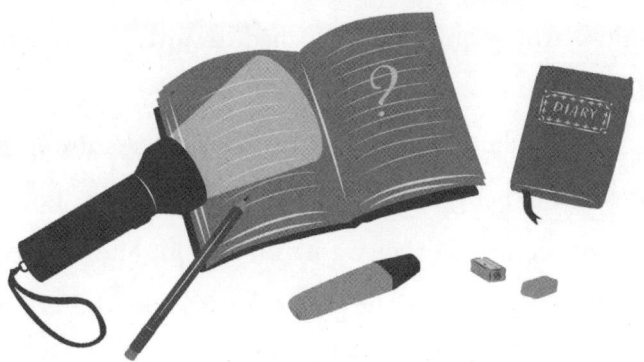

Grace hung up, her heart pounding. Her brain was paralysed with fear. She was motionless for a moment, then the adrenaline kicked in.

She silently clambered onto the chest of drawers and pulled open the sash window. The roof of the kitchen extension was just below, and Grace stepped carefully onto its sloped surface before leaning back inside to grab the plastic bag containing last night's discovery. As she did, her phone slipped out of her hand

and tumbled onto her bedroom floor. Grace briefly considered climbing back inside to get it, but a noise from below told her there was no time. She had to get out. Turning quickly, she inched towards the edge of the roof.

When she got there, she hesitated. If she dropped down into her garden, then whoever was in the house might see her, so that wasn't an option. She glanced over to her next-door neighbour's garden to the left. It was far less overgrown than hers, and a path of paving stones led to the back gate which opened on to the alley at the back of the houses. She couldn't see if the gate was locked but she'd have to try it. There was no other way.

Grace silently crept across the roof and placed her free hand on the fence, crying out as an exposed nail tore into her palm. Gritting her teeth, she vaulted over, landing softly on the other side. She sprinted to the back gate, yanked it open and risked a quick glance back at her house.

A man was climbing out of her bedroom window,

his face concealed by a balaclava.

Grace ran into the alley and was immediately met by Suzy.

'Quick! This way!' Suzy said, pulling Grace down the alley towards the high street. 'We can't go to mine. Mum and Dad are out and whoever's after you might know where I live. We'd be sitting ducks. We need to get somewhere where there are people,' Suzy gasped as they ran. 'Do you have your phone? We need to call the police.'

Grace shook her head, 'No. We'll have to call them at the first shop we get to.'

They turned the corner to the high street but, too late, Grace remembered it was Sunday. They wouldn't be open for another thirty minutes! Cursing their foolishness, she looked in each of the windows they passed, willing there to be someone inside.

They were all empty.

Until they reached Mrs Peel's shop.

As they ran past, Scruff bounded to the inside of the door and barked a greeting.

'Look, Suze! Mrs P's in,' Grace cried, skidding to a halt. Just inside, Mrs Peel was busy filling buckets of flowers, her back to the door. Grace and Suzy pounded their fists on the glass.

'Mrs Peel!' Grace shouted. 'Mrs Peel! Let us in! Mrs Peel!'

Inside, Mrs Peel didn't turn around. Then Grace spotted the fine cable hanging down from her ears.

She had headphones in.

Grace frantically looked down the road for anyone they could run to for help. But at that moment, the man from her house rounded the corner on to the end of the high street. He immediately caught sight of Grace and Suzy and sprinted along the pavement towards them.

Grace stepped up her banging. Mrs Peel just *had* to hear them. She *had* to!

Inside the shop, Mrs Peel turned to fill another bucket and caught the movement outside the shop. Frowning, she removed her earphones and walked towards the door. Then she spotted the terrified expressions on the girls' faces and ran the last few steps. She unlocked the door and Grace and Suzy tumbled inside.

'Quick, lock the door!' Grace shouted at the shocked woman. Mrs Peel immediately twisted the lock and stepped away from the door.

'What's going on? What's wrong? You look like you've seen a ghost!' she asked. Then she noticed Grace's hand. 'And you're bleeding!'

'No time,' Grace panted, clutching her hand to her chest. 'We need to hide.'

'But–'

'Mrs Peel. Listen to me. There's a man after us. We need to hide!' Suzy said, willing the woman to believe her.

Mrs Peel didn't hesitate.

She moved quickly to the side of the front door and pushed a switch high up on the wall. Immediately, the whirr of a motor sounded and the metal shutter that covered the front of the shop slowly lowered. Then she pushed a red button just below the switch and turned back to the girls.

'Follow me,' she said, leading them towards the back

of the shop to a flight of wooden stairs.

BANG!

Grace spun around at the sound of the man banging his fist on the metal shutter. It had already lowered to cover the top half of the door, and Grace could just see his legs and waist. But he wasn't giving up that easily. As she watched, he bent and picked a stone up off the ground and started hammering it against the shutter. The metal bent alarmingly, but held in place.

But for how long, she didn't know.

CHAPTER 27

Grace turned and hurried after the others, who had already made it to the top of the stairs. By the time she'd reached the top, Mrs Peel had grabbed a pole with a small hook on the end and was reaching up to a hatch in the ceiling. She slotted the hook into a metal ring and pulled. The hatch lowered and a ladder slid down from the opening.

'Up there. Quick,' Mrs Peel whispered, guiding Grace forwards. Grace gripped the plastic bag between her teeth and began to climb. Suzy was right behind her, followed by Mrs Peel and Scruff, who was lying precariously over the woman's right shoulder.

When Mrs Peel climbed off the top rung of the ladder, she quickly reached down and pulled the hatch up with the pole then gestured for them to follow her into the eaves at the far end of the attic space.

Downstairs, the banging stopped.

'Right, what's going on?' she whispered.

'It's the coat ... the new one ... visions ... Liv was murdered ... we've been investigating ... now someone's after us,' Grace panted, barely coherent. She could tell straight away from the expression on Mrs Peel's face that she didn't believe her.

'Come on now, what's really going on?' Mrs Peel asked.

Grace grabbed the plastic bag. 'Look,' she said, holding it towards Mrs Peel. The woman untied the knot and glanced inside then immediately shut the bag.

'Is that what I think it is?' she asked.

'Yes.' Grace turned to Suzy. 'I didn't get the chance

to tell you, but I found the murder site and visited it yesterday. There was a rose bush planted at the exact spot I'd drawn in the sketch of my visions. I dug and found these.'

'You mean?' Suzy asked.

Grace nodded. 'I've found her, Suze. I've found Liv.'

Just then, the sound of splintering wood came from the back of the shop. Grace had seen enough detective shows to recognise the unmistakable sound of the lock being broken off the back door. Scruff barked and ran to the hatch.

'Scruff, get back here!' Mrs Peel hissed. The dog immediately came scurrying back, hearing the fear in his owner's voice. 'Good boy,' she whispered, wrapping her arms around him to make sure he didn't dart away again. The three held their breath as they listened carefully.

Silence filled the air as they waited. *He must be checking out downstairs*, Grace realised.

Creak!

Creak!

Creak!

He was walking upstairs! Grace glanced at the others, who were staring wide-eyed at the hatch.

A door below them clicked open. Footsteps moved around the room then out onto the landing space again.

He's checking the rooms!

Grace turned to Mrs Peel. 'How many rooms are there up here?' she whispered.

'Three,' Mrs Peel replied. 'Don't worry though, the police will be here soon. That red button by the front door sends an emergency signal to the local station. They fitted it after there was a spate of robberies a few years back, though I hoped I'd never have to use it,' she added.

Grace desperately hoped she was right as a soft *click* from below signalled that the man had moved into the second room.

The footsteps grew quieter as they moved around the room at the far end, then louder as the man walked onto the landing again.

Click.

Room number three.

There were a few moments of silence, then the attacker's footsteps returned to the landing.

'I know you're here!' the man's voice called out. Grace immediately recognised that voice. Frank May. 'You might as well make it easy on yourself and come out now.' The pacing below them continued, growing louder then quieter as Frank walked the length of the landing. The footsteps then stopped.

Right below the hatch.

CHAPTER 28

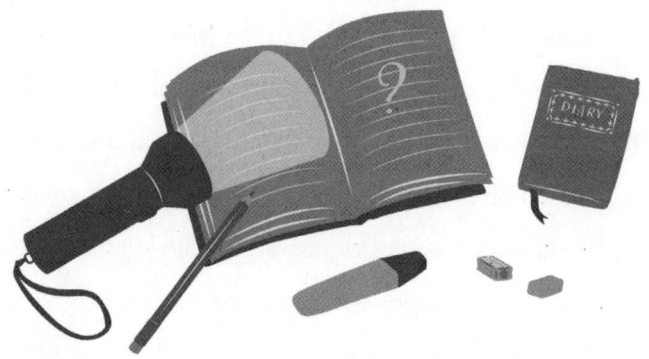

'Really? You thought you'd hide in the attic? Where did you think you'd go from there?' Frank gave a humourless chuckle. 'Well, stay where you are. I'll be up in just a minute.'

His footsteps moved away from the hatch again and the shriek of wood on wood shattered the silence. Something heavy was being dragged across the floor to the point directly under the hatch.

'Last chance. Come down and I'll go easy on you.'

His words were like a shard of ice in Grace's heart. Frank was right. There was nowhere they could go from their position in the attic.

'Get behind me, girls,' Mrs Peel said, moving forwards.

'No chance, Mrs P,' Suzy shot back as she grabbed an old chair leg off the floor and wielded it like a bat.

'She's right,' Grace agreed, taking hold of an old iron lamp. 'It's three against one. Whatever happens, *we're* not going to go easy on *him*!'

Mrs Peel smiled nervously and took hold of a pottery garden gnome.

There was a rattle as the hatch mechanism was pulled down.

'Ready?' Mrs Peel whispered.

'Ready!' the girls replied in unison.

Just then there was a screech of brakes outside the shop, followed by the slamming of car doors. 'Round the back!' a man's voice barked and footsteps thumped around the building.

Frank cursed, and his footsteps receded. Grace, Suzy and Mrs Peel didn't move. For a moment, nothing

happened, but then there was an explosion of activity from below as a scuffle broke out.

Footsteps once again headed towards the loft hatch.

'Mrs Peel? Are you up there? This is the police. We've caught the intruder, and you're safe to come down now,' came a man's voice from below them.

Grace lowered herself down the ladder first and was immediately hustled out of the shop to a waiting ambulance by two armed officers.

A young female paramedic wearing a badge with Nicola written on it stepped towards Grace. 'What've we got?'

'Superficial wound to the hand,' one of the officers replied before turning and heading back into the shop.

'What's your name, love?' Nicola asked.

'Grace.'

'Okay, Grace. Let's take a look at your hand.' She carefully eased it open. 'That's not too bad, I'll just need to give it a clean and dress it, then you'll be good to go.'

Grace winced as the paramedic rinsed the wound with antiseptic before applying a dressing. 'Just hold that for me a sec, and I'll tape it in place,' Nicola instructed, placing Grace's hand on top of the dressing. A few moments later, she was all taped up. 'How're you feeling apart from your hand?'

'Okay,' Grace replied.

'Right then, I think there's a gentleman over there who'd like a word with you.' Nicola gestured to a dark-haired man wearing a grey suit and striped tie who was standing in front of the ambulance. He was handing an evidence bag containing Grace's plastic bag with the bottle and bone in to one of the armed officers.

Grace stood and made her way over. The man smiled as she approached and introduced himself.

'Hi Grace, I'm Detective Sergeant Gonzales. We're going to take you to the station to find out what happened here. Do you have someone we can call to come with you?'

'My mum, but she's been away at a conference and might not be back yet,' Grace replied.

'Not to worry. We'll give her a quick call to let her know what's happened and where we're taking you so she can pop by when she's back. Is there anyone else you'd like us to call to come with you?'

'No, I'm fine. Can my friend Suzy come in with me?' Grace asked.

'I'm afraid not. We'll need to speak to you both separately. We can wait for your mum to arrive if you'd like?' the detective asked.

Grace thought about everything that had happened over the last week, and everything that she'd done. There was no way she wanted her mum hearing every last detail!

'It's okay, I don't need my mum there.'

DS Gonzales nodded. He led Grace to the rear of the squad car and opened the door. Once Grace was safely inside, he walked to the front of the vehicle and got in.

Grace had never been in a police car before and was surprised to find it was almost identical to her mum's car. She'd expected plastic covered seats and maybe a cage or plastic screen between the rear and front seats like you got in American police series, but there was nothing like that.

When they arrived at the station, DS Gonzales led Grace over to a reception desk. 'Grace Yi regarding the incident at Flower Power. We'll need a room,' he said to the officer behind the desk.

'No problem, I'll check for you now,' the officer replied, then tapped a few keys on the computer in front of him. 'Interview Room 3 is free. You can head straight on in.'

'Thanks.' DS Gonzales turned to Grace. 'This way.' He led her into a small room with whitewashed walls. Against one wall, was a rectangular wooden table with two blue padded chairs at either side. 'Take a seat, Grace. Would you like a drink of water before we start?'

'No, I'm fine thanks,' she said, eager to get it over with.

'Great. I need to make you aware that this interview will be recorded, are you okay with that?'

Grace nodded.

'Okay, let's get started then,' DS Gonzales said. 'Grace, could you tell me, in your own words, what

happened today. Try not to leave out any information, even if it seems really insignificant. Small things can sometimes be the difference between us solving a case or not.'

'Well, it all began just over a week ago …'

Grace told him about what had happened. About the coat and the visions. The research and the meetings. The man following her and the missing phone and keys. The possible murder sites and the rose bush. The bones and the bottle. And finally, Frank at the florist's. When she'd finished, DS Gonzales sat back in his chair.

'That's some story, Grace,' he said, running a hand through his hair. 'Just to make sure I've got this right. You bought a coat, then got visions when you put it on. In one of the visions, you saw a girl murdered. You then investigated, talked to some of the girl's old classmates and solved the murder. From those same visions, you managed to find the scene of the murder but got chased by a man who isn't the murderer but is covering up for them. Does that about sum it up?'

Grace could tell he didn't believe her. If she hadn't

lived through it herself, *she* wouldn't believe her either. 'Really!' she said. 'I know it seems far-fetched but check the bone. Surely you'll be able to get DNA or something from it. And find the rose bush. If you dig there, you'll find the rest of Liv's remains, and that'll prove what I'm saying,' she blustered. 'And—' DS Gonzales held his hand up to silence Grace.

'Don't worry, we'll do all of that. And we've got Mr May in custody, so we'll see what he's got to say too. Rest assured—'

A knock on the door interrupted him, and a female officer poked her head around the door. 'Grace's mum is here, shall I bring her in?'

DS Gonzales nodded and moments later, Grace's mum burst into the room and embraced her.

'Are you alright?' she asked, looking over every part of Grace as if needing to see with her own eyes that she was okay.

'I'm fine, Mum. Really.'

Mrs Yi looked over to DS Gonzales.

'She's been seen by paramedics and, aside from a cut

on her hand, she's fine,' he said. 'We've got the attacker in custody, Mrs Yi, but as a precaution I'm going to post a couple of officers outside your house until we get to the bottom of what happened today.'

'Officers? Do you think she's still at risk?' Grace's mum asked, her eyes still wide with shock.

'Not necessarily, but we don't want to take any risks at this stage. I'm sure Grace will fill you in on everything when you get home, but for now, try not to worry. We'll update you when we know anything more.' DS Gonzales walked to the door. 'Here's my card. Call me if Grace remembers anything she might have missed today or if you're worried about anything at all.' He opened the door and led Grace and her mum to the front door of the station.

Grace's mum's car was parked directly outside, and she unlocked it without saying a word. She broke her silence only when they got inside.

'Grace Yi, you have *a lot* of explaining to do …'

CHAPTER 29

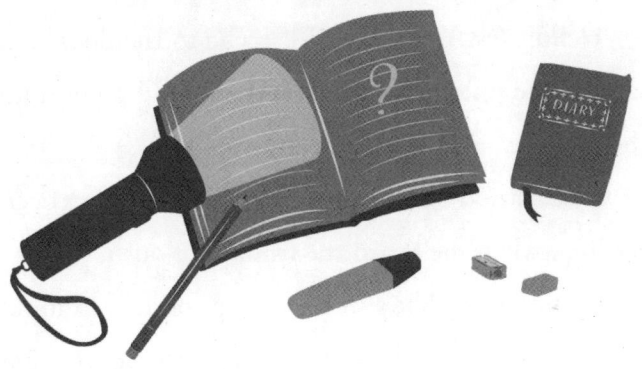

For the next two days, Grace didn't leave the house at all. Her mum had shut all the curtains and locked all the doors and had banned Grace from using her phone – even to talk to Suzy. 'You don't know who might be listening, Grace. You said someone had managed to track what you were doing so they could have tampered with your phone. It's not worth the risk for a couple of days stuck in the house,' she'd explained when Grace complained for the millionth time about how unfair it was. 'It won't be for long.'

And she was right. At 6pm on the second day, the phone rang. Grace's mum answered it.

'Hello? Yes. Yes. Okay, I'll come to the door,' she said before putting the phone down and going into the hallway.

Grace stood up from the sofa, where she'd been reading, when she heard the front door open.

'Come on in. She's in the living room,' her mum said. The door to the living room opened and DS Gonzales walked in. He nodded a greeting to Grace then turned to her mum. 'We've had a breakthrough in the case, and I wanted to update you in person. Could I take a seat?' he asked.

'Oh, of course.' Grace's mum gestured for him to sit, and DS Gonzales lowered himself into an armchair opposite the sofa.

Grace sat back down.

'So,' DS Gonzales began, 'my team has been to the location where you said you'd dug up the bone and have found the remains of a female. From the size of the bones, it looks to be a juvenile, but we'll know more once the labs have run tests. Frank May has admitted to breaking into your house and the florist's but denies murdering Olivia Montague.'

Grace leant forwards in her seat. 'Did you speak to Mr Bainbridge?'

DS Gonzales nodded. 'Yes, he was interviewed by officers in London and confirmed that Olivia used to date Frank, and when she decided to date Mr Bainbridge instead, Mr May flew into a jealous rage, stalking her and refusing to accept that she'd left him. When Olivia disappeared, Mr Bainbridge assumed she'd left because it was all getting too much for her.'

'But that's not right. Mr Bainbridge killed Liv. He must have!' Grace cried out in disbelief.

DS Gonzales held up a hand. 'I know what you thought you saw in your visions, Grace, but the facts speak for themselves. Frank chased after you because you'd found out his secret. Plus, we've checked the CCTV footage from the charity shop you bought your coat from, and we can clearly see Frank deposit the bike with the coat in the basket the day before you bought it. Although the lab is doubtful they'll get any DNA evidence from the bottle, we're confident we should have enough to charge Mr May with Olivia's murder.'

'But what about the diary? Johnny met with Liv on the day she went missing. I bet he didn't tell you that!' Grace said, pulling the diary out of her pocket and holding it out to the detective.

'Grace, we've arrested the killer. Now, we'll keep the patrol car with you until we're sure we've got a cast iron case against Mr May. We know he's got links with some very unsavoury characters, so we'd like you to stay inside for a little while longer.'

Grace sat in stunned silence. They'd arrested the wrong man!

DS Gonzales stood up and turned to Grace. 'I've got to say I was a bit sceptical of your story, with the coat and the visions and everything else. But you've done a remarkable job and solved a case from over fifty years ago. There are not many detectives who could do that.' He smiled. 'I'll see myself out.' The detective walked out of the room, and Grace heard the front door close softly behind him.

'Mum, what time is it?' Grace asked.

Her mum checked her watch. '2:30. Why?'

'I need to tell Suzy what's happened! I'm going up to my room to message her,' Grace said before racing out of the living room and up the stairs. When she got to her bedroom, she walked straight to her bedroom window to check whether Suzy was there or not. She wasn't.

Over the last few days, unable to speak to each other by phone, Grace and Suzy had taken to using Morse code again to communicate every day at 10am, 3pm and 8pm so she had thirty minutes to wait.

Sighing with impatience, Grace grabbed her sketchbook. The image of Liv, smiling as she left the house on that fateful day all those years ago, appeared in her mind. She immediately began to sketch, trying her best to capture the slightly mischievous sparkle in her eyes and the sheer joy on her face. Grace had just finished her rough sketch when a glimmer of light caught her eye. She placed the sketchbook on her bed and stepped over to the window. It was Suzy. Grace picked up her torch and turned it on.

.... ..

(Hi)

--. ..- . ... / .-- .... .- -

(Guess what)?

.- .-. .-. . ... - . -.. / ..-. / ....- / .-.. / -- ..- .-. -.. . .-.

(Arrested F 4 L murder)

There was a slight pause, then a series of flashes came from Suzy's window.

.-- .... .- -

(What)?

Grace messaged back.

.. / -.- -. --- .--

(I know)!

... - .. .-.. .-.. / --. --- - / - --- / ... - .- -.-- / .. -. / - .... ---

(Still got to stay in tho)

Suzy's flashes came immediately back.

-. .. --. .... - -- .- -.- .

(Nightmare)

-. . . -.. / - --- / .-. .-. --- ...- . / .--- /

-.- .. .-.. .-.. . .-.

(Need to prove J killer)

.-- .. .-.. .-.. / - .... .. -. -.-

(Will think)

-.-. / ..- / .- - / ---..

(CU at 8)?

-.-. / ..- / .- - / ---..

(CU at 8) Grace replied.

She waved and put the torch back next to the window for later and got back to her sketch.

CHAPTER 30

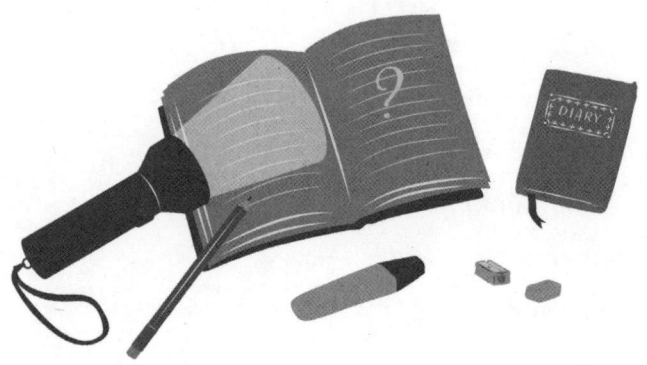

Johnny picked up his phone and called.

'Yes?'

'Marco, it's Mr Bainbridge. You've been doing a job for me.'

'Yes, sir.'

'Frank has become … indisposed, so I'll take over things from here. You still have eyes and ears on the girls I take it?'

'Yes, sir. Their phones are off, but I still have access to

their laptop audio and searches.'

'Good. I need to be informed immediately if there is any mention of me by name in conversation or in any searches. And I mean immediately. This is of the utmost importance. Understand?'

'Yes, sir. I'll let you know.'

Johnny hung up and sat back in his chair. The case against Frank was 100% solid, he'd made sure of that.

And he was going to make sure it stayed that way.

CHAPTER 31

The next morning, Grace's mum called her into her study. 'I know I probably don't even need to ask, but would you like to invite Suzy over? I've spoken to her parents and they're happy to drop her round as long as you both stay in the house and they pick her back up afterwards.'

'Yes, yes, yes!' Grace squealed. 'Can she come over right away?'

Grace's mum laughed. 'Of course. I'll call her

parents now.'

'Thanks, Mum, you're the best!' Grace dashed out of the room to get dressed and was back downstairs just as the doorbell rang.

'I'll get it!' her mum called, hurrying out of her office. She pulled open the door. 'Hi Bob. Suzy, do you want to go on in? Grace is desperate to see you.'

'Thanks, Mrs Yi.' Suzy grinned, jogging over to Grace who was standing at the bottom of the stairs.

'It feels like forever since I saw you!' Grace said, hugging Suzy fiercely. 'Come on up.' They went up to Grace's bedroom and flopped on the bed.

'So, they arrested Frank. I take it you told them it wasn't him who killed Liv?'

'Of course. But they didn't believe me because all the evidence points to Frank.' Grace sighed. 'And in all honesty, if I were them, I wouldn't believe it was Johnny either.'

'Not yet, anyway,' Suzy said. 'There must be *something* we've missed to tie Johnny to the murder. We just haven't spotted it.'

'Suze. We've looked at everything a million times and haven't found anything to tie him to Liv's murder.'

'Looking one more time won't harm then. Pull together everything we've discovered so far and we'll go through it with a fine-tooth comb.'

Grace grabbed her laptop, Liv's diary and the notes she'd made after the vision of Liv's murder and spread them out on her bed. 'Okay, so let's start with the diary,' she said, but it soon became clear there was nothing to help them there. 'It's no good. It's all in code and obviously there's no entry after Liv met Johnny that last time.'

'Okay,' Suzy said. 'Let's take a look at your notes.'

* **Girl: Liv (Olivia) – rich – big house, chandelier, grand piano in sitting room, gold curtains, high ceilings.**
* **Boy: Johnny – older?**
* **Met on open grassland. Couldn't be far from home – Liv cycled there.**
* **What happened to the bike?**

'Hmmm. Not a lot there either. There *must* have

been something else though,' Suzy said. 'Tell you what, why don't you try and tell me what you saw to see if anything rings alarm bells.'

'Okay.' Grace closed her eyes. 'So Liv was standing next to Johnny. She told him she couldn't stay long because she was expected at Georgina's house, and Johnny wasn't happy. He had a go at her for not stealing money too. His parents had cut off his allowance, so he was broke. Liv wouldn't stay though and ended up breaking up with him. When she tried to walk away, he grabbed her but she pushed him away and ran off. Johnny stumbled backwards and the cola bottle he'd been holding broke and cut his hand. Liv went back to see if he was okay and he hit her with the broken bottle.' Grace opened her eyes. 'That's it.'

Suzy was silent as she thought about what Grace had said. 'Hang on. You said Johnny cut his hand?' Grace nodded. 'How bad was it?'

'Pretty bad. There was blood running down his arm.'

'That's it then! That's the thing that's going to tie Johnny to the murder!'

'What're you talking about? What's him cutting his hand got to do with anything?' Grace asked.

'Don't you see? He'd have needed to go to a doctor or to the hospital to get the cut seen to. If the police track down his medical records, then they'll see he had an injury the day Liv died!'

Grace took a moment to absorb what her friend had said but then slowly nodded. 'You could be right, Suze. It'd certainly make DS Gonzales look into him a bit more, *and* he'd need a good excuse for how he cut his hand on the day Liv was murdered. Let's go get his number off Mum, and we'll call him now!'

The girls ran downstairs to the office. 'Mum, can I have DS Gonzales's business card? We've just thought of something he might need to know.'

Grace's mum looked up from her work. 'Oh yes, what have you found?'

Grace hesitated, unsure of how much to tell her mum. If she told her about Johnny's hand, would she try to stop them calling the detective? She needn't have worried as Suzy cut in, 'Grace has remembered a small detail from her vision that might help secure Frank's arrest. It's only a little thing, but they do say the smallest thing can sometimes be the most important.'

Grace's mum hesitated for a moment, but then reached into the top drawer of her desk and pulled out his business card.

'Thanks, Mum!' Grace said. She grabbed the house phone and took it up to her bedroom, then dialled the number on the card.

'DS Golzales.'

'Hi DS Gonzales. It's Grace Yi.'

'Oh, hi Grace. What can I do for you?'

'I've remembered something about Liv's murder. Something that proves that Jonathan Bainbridge had something to do with her death.'

'Okay,' DS Gonzales said with a hint of a sigh. 'What've you got?'

'Well, Johnny cut his hand when he killed Liv. If you check his medical records, you'll find he had treatment for the wound on the day Liv disappeared.' Grace winced. It had seemed like such strong evidence when she and Suzy had talked about it, but now she felt a little foolish.

'And you think this will prove he killed Liv?' the detective said. 'Sorry, Grace. It's a cut and dried case. Frank killed Liv, and if Jonathan Bainbridge cut his hand, then that's all it was. A cut. You've got to drop this. Okay?' He sounded cross.

'Okay. Sorry to have bothered you,' Grace muttered, ending the call.

'He didn't believe you, did he?' Suzy asked.

'No. He didn't.'

CHAPTER 32

Johnny's phone rang.

'Yes.'

'It's Marco. It's probably nothing, but the girls were in Grace's bedroom and they had the weirdest conversation. I wasn't sure whether to bother you with it, but you said I was to call if I heard your name mentioned.'

'Go on,' Johnny encouraged.

'Like I said, it was weird. One of them started talking about a vision of some girl being killed and they were *saying you did it and you cut your hand on a bottle. They got really excited and called the police to tell them you'd done it. I couldn't hear the full conversation, but from the side of it I could hear, it didn't sound like the guy they called believed them. And who can blame him right?' Marco laughed.*

'Right, thanks Marco. Keep listening.'

Johnny hung up and sat back in his chair. How did the girl know about his hand? And if she really did have a vision, then she was dangerous.

Too dangerous to be allowed to run around pointing fingers.

He pressed the intercom on his desk.

'Sandra, cancel my meetings. I'm going to be out of the office for the rest of the day.'

CHAPTER 33

'Grace! Your tea's ready!' Grace's mum called after Suzy had left.

Grace ran downstairs to the kitchen, where her mum was laying out an Indian banquet. 'Ooh, Indian! We never have Indian!' Grace said quickly stepping over to the kitchen island and lifting lids to look.

'Well, it is a celebration after all,' her mum said. 'The police have caught the killer *and*, after the detective's visit, I had a call from the office. I got the promotion!'

She grinned.

'Oh Mum! Congratulations! That's amazing!' Grace squealed, hugging her and jumping up and down.

'I know! So, I've got all your favourites: butter chicken, lamb balti, pilau rice, peshwari naan and poppadoms with a chutney and pickle tray.' She paused. 'And I got you this.' She pulled a piece of paper from her pocket and held it out to Grace.

'What is it?' she asked, unfolding it.

'Read it and you'll find out!' Her mum laughed.

Grace couldn't believe her eyes.

It was a printed receipt for a place on the art course.

'You mean …?'

Her mum nodded, grinning. 'I knew you'd been saving to go and, what with having to buy the coat, I figured you might need a hand paying for it. And with the bonus that comes with the promotion, you can go on as many courses and buy as many coats as you want!'

'Thank you, thank you, thank you!' Grace said, hugging her mum again, unable to believe she was actually booked on the course.

'Now, let's eat before it goes cold. Could you grab a couple of plates and cutlery and I'll get the rest out?' her mum asked, pulling another steaming tray out of the oven.

Grace grabbed everything they needed and perched on one of the stools. Then she piled her plate high with food.

'Mum?' she asked, her mouth full of rice.

'Grace!'

'Sorry,' she mumbled, swallowing. 'Do you fancy a film while we eat? I've seen there are some new ones on Netflix this week.'

'Good plan. Let's go through to the living room. We can always come back in here to top up our plates.' Her mum picked up her plate and led the way into the living room. 'Right, let's see what we've got,' she said, flicking through the possible films. 'Any preference?'

'Anything but murder mysteries. I've had enough of those to last me a lifetime!' Grace joked.

'Deal. Let's go for a romcom then. We've not had one of those for ages.' She selected a film, and they settled down to watch it.

The film was alright. It was the typical boy meets girl stuff, but it filled the time. When it was over, Grace turned to her mum. 'Is it okay if I go upstairs for a bit? I want to finish a sketch before I talk to Suzy?'

'Yeah, of course you can. Just take your plate through to the kitchen, and I'll do the rest.' No sooner had she finished speaking, the phone rang. Grace's mum crossed the room and picked it up from next to the sofa.

'Hello? Hello? Oh, hello, DS Gonzales. Sorry, can you just speak up a bit, it's a terrible line. Yes. Yes. No, that's fine. Of course he can. I'll just let her know. Pardon? Okay. What's his name? Great. Thanks for letting me know. Bye.' She hung up. 'That was DS Gonzales. One of his constables will be coming round soon to ask you a few more questions about Frank May. It was an awful line, but I think he said it'll be Constable White. You go on up, and I'll let you know when he gets here.'

'Thanks, Mum!' she replied before heading upstairs.

She needn't have bothered. She'd hardly opened her sketchbook when the doorbell rang.

'Grace! Constable White's here!' her mum shouted up the stairs.

'Coming, Mum,' Grace replied, checking her clock. 7:45pm – only fifteen minutes before Suzy would be at her window. *I hope it's quick*, she thought as she made her way down the stairs. When she was halfway down, she could just make out snippets of conversation from below. The constable's voice was oddly familiar, but Grace couldn't quite place it. *Maybe he's one of the officers from the night Frank chased me?*

As she rounded the bottom, she saw the policeman in the hallway with his back to her as he spoke to her mum. Grace fleetingly noticed that his uniform was ill-fitting and looked like it had been made for someone much bigger, but it was his voice that caught her attention. She frowned as something niggled at the back of her mind, something just out of reach.

Where *did* she know that voice from?

Before she'd had any chance to work it out, Grace's mum spotted her at the bottom of the stairs. 'Ah, here she is. Grace, this is Constable White.'

The policeman turned his head to look at her, and she immediately knew where she'd heard that voice.

She would recognise those cold grey eyes anywhere.

It was Jonathan Bainbridge.

CHAPTER 34

'Hello Grace.' He smiled.

Grace froze to the spot, her brain struggling to comprehend what she was seeing. Before she could react, Johnny lurched to his left, grabbing an ornament from the hall table. In one swift movement, he brought it crashing down on her mum's head, and she fell to the floor, a large gash on her temple already oozing bright red blood.

Grace hesitated for a split second before racing up

the stairs. She'd be no use to her mum if Johnny got hold of her too. But Johnny was faster than he looked. He lunged at her, grabbing her ankle as she took the first of the steps and yanking it towards him, sending Grace sprawling onto the stairs.

'Don't be silly, girl. You can't get awa … oof!' he cried out as she kicked out at him. Grace immediately scrambled away and raced up the stairs.

'Where are you running to, Grace? You wouldn't leave your mum to bleed out on the floor, would you?' His words tore through Grace's heart, but she knew she had to get away to make sure that *didn't* happen. His footsteps were slow and steady as he followed her up the stairs.

He knew he didn't need to run.

She was trapped.

As soon as Grace reached the top of the stairs, she sprinted across the landing and yanked open the bathroom door. She slammed it shut behind her and tugged the bolt closed.

Desperately, she looked around for a weapon – or

anything she could use against Johnny – but there was nothing. Nothing to barricade the door with either.

She really *was* trapped.

Grace perched on the edge of the bath and thought. There had to be a way of getting out and saving her mum! Then she spotted the candle her mum used when she was in the bath. Maybe … just maybe … The rattle of the door handle broke into Grace's thoughts as Johnny tried to force the door open.

'You might as well come out, Grace,' he said, as the door rattled on its hinges. It held shut. But only just.

Grace snatched up the candle, placed it on the windowsill and lit it with a match. The window was frosted, but she was pretty sure the flame would be visible from outside. She just had to hope Suzy was looking her way.

She grabbed a towel and placed it between the candle and the glass before raising and lowering it in a pattern.

… --- …
… --- …

... --- ...

... --- ...

... --- ...

... --- ...

She waited.

But there was no reply from Suzy, and, with a deafening crash, Johnny shoulder barged the door and came hurtling into the bathroom. There was nowhere for Grace to go. She tried to dodge past him, but he caught hold of her arm and pulled her out of the bathroom and down the stairs.

When they reached the bottom, Grace immediately looked to where her mum had fallen. She was still there. Blood pooled on the floor by her head and her face was now waxy and pallid.

'Mum!' Grace cried out, trying to pull away. But Johnny's grip was firm.

'Not so fast. You're coming with me. You'll be reunited with your mum later,' he snarled as he dragged her into the kitchen. When they reached the island counter, Johnny pulled a pair of cable tie handcuffs from his belt.

'Sit,' he ordered, pushing Grace to the floor. He quickly placed a cuff over one of her wrists then leant down to pull it around the back of one of the legs of the island. Grace saw her chance. She snatched her bound hand away and toppled her full weight forwards onto Johnny's back. He tumbled forwards onto the floor, landing with a grunt.

Grace leapt to her feet.

Aiming a swift kick at his ribs, she sprinted into the hallway to the front door. Her stomach twisted as she ran past her mum, but she had to get out. Had to get help.

Reaching the door, she yanked on the handle.

Nothing happened.

A small sob escaped her lips as she pulled with all her might. But it was no good.

The door was locked.

'You'll be needing these.'

Grace spun round.

Johnny stood at the bottom of the stairs, the front

door keys swinging from his fingers. Grace desperately searched for a way to escape, but his large frame filled the hallway.

He stepped forwards, closing the gap between them, and Grace pressed her back against the door.

'There's nowhere to go. It's over.'

Grace opened her mouth to scream for help, but before she could make a sound, Johnny's hand clamped over her mouth and his arm snaked around her neck. She twisted and kicked and hit, but he was too strong and easily pushed her back to the kitchen. By the time he lowered her next to the kitchen island again, stars were dancing at the edge of her vision as she fought for breath.

This time, when Johnny bent to tie the cuff around the leg of the island, all Grace could do was suck in rasping lungfuls of air. After one final tug on her ties to make sure they were secure, Johnny stood.

'Now to check on your mum. We can't have her waking up and ruining everything, can we?' he said, and walked towards the hallway.

'Leave her alone! Why are you doing this?' Grace gasped, clawing uselessly at her binds.

Johnny turned and strode over to Grace. He pulled a handkerchief from his pocket and tied it around her mouth.

'There, that's better,' he said, and left the room.

Tears coursed down Grace's cheeks as she watched him leave. She listened for any sign of what was happening but was met with only silence. Was her mum even *alive*?

Then Johnny walked back into the kitchen and glanced over at Grace. 'Don't worry, she's still breathing. For now, anyway,' he said, seeming to read her thoughts. 'You had to dig around, didn't you? You just couldn't leave it alone. That was a *big* mistake.'

He rummaged in his trouser pocket and pulled out a silver cigarette lighter. 'Not to worry though. It'll all be over soon. I'll tie up any loose ends that might incriminate me, and then life will go back to normal …' He paused. 'For me anyway. And I'll be able to forget all about Olivia Montague again,' he added cheerfully as he walked around the room, removing the keys from the back door and windows before lowering the roller blind so no one could see inside. 'There we go. Nice and private. Goodbye, Grace Yi.'

And with that, he left the room and walked into the dining room that adjoined the kitchen at the back of the house. Moments later, she heard Johnny's footsteps on the laminate floor of the hallway and the faint click of the front door followed shortly after.

Grace didn't wait. She spat out the gag and pulled at her bonds with renewed energy, calling out to her mum to try and stir her into consciousness, but there was no response.

'Don't worry, Mum. I'll get us out of here,' she called out as she stretched a foot towards the cutlery drawer. As she did, her body twisted towards the dining room and terror clutched at her chest. Tendrils of smoke were curling under the bottom of the door.

Johnny had set a fire.

Grace redoubled her efforts but no matter how much she stretched she just couldn't reach.

'Come on, Mum. We've got to get out of here. Mum, I need your help! I can't do this by myself!' Grace sobbed as she realised there was no way out. She tried to tuck her nose and mouth into the top of her t-shirt. It was no use. Choking smoke was now filling the room and she struggled for breath.

She glanced towards the hallway. There were still no signs of movement from her mum. She *had* to do something!

Grace twisted and tugged and pulled over and over again, her actions getting slower and slower as the smoke filled her lungs.

Until there was only blackness.

CHAPTER 35

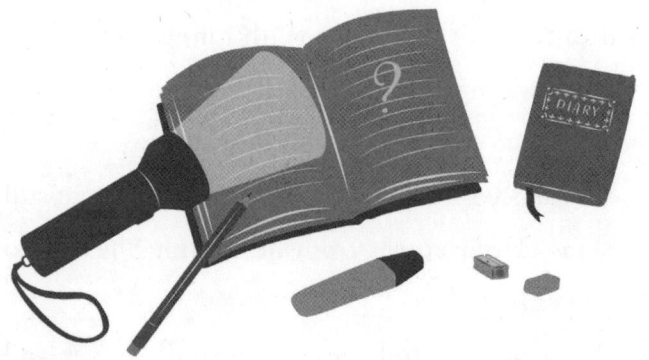

'Grace! Grace!' The voice sounded a million miles away.

'Grace! Wake up, Grace!' The sound tugged at her mind, but she was so tired.

No, she couldn't be tired. She had to save her mum!

Grace's mind clawed its way through the fog that blanketed it. It reached out, towards the faint glow just beyond.

'Grace? Hey, she's coming round!' The voice again.

Grace knew she had to make her way towards that voice. She fought to raise her eyelids, but they were leaden, demanding to be kept closed. Ignoring their protests, she dragged them open, millimetre by millimetre until she saw a sight that made her heart burst.

Her mum was propped up against a tree in the garden, a tea towel pressed to her forehead. And she was awake!

Grace struggled to move. 'Whoa there, Grace,' came the voice again. A voice she was so glad to hear.

'Suzy!' Grace spluttered as a coughing fit took over her.

'The one and only,' Suzy tried to sound light-hearted, but Grace could hear the strain in her voice, even in her foggy state. 'You've got to stay still. We've called for help, and they should be here any minute.'

'Johnny?' Grace whispered, her head beginning to clear.

'Gone. After I saw your message, Mum called the police while me and Dad raced round. Dad was *amazing*. He vaulted over your back gate like it was nothing and kicked in the back door just like you see in Hollywood films!' Suzy glanced at the shattered planks of wood that used to be Grace's back door. 'Um, yeah. So, you'll be needing a new back door …'

Grace smiled at the thought of Suzy's quiet beauty therapist dad karate kicking her back door down. 'I don't think Mum will mind that too much. You saved us, Suzy. I really thought we'd …' Grace's voice tailed off, unable to finish the sentence.

'Well, if it hadn't been for your quick thinking with the Morse code you might have been.' Suzy's eyes glistened at the thought, and she took off her glasses and wiped at them with the back of her hand.

Outside the house, the blare of sirens grew closer. Doors slammed and suddenly the garden was filled with people, all shouting instructions. A paramedic raced to Grace's side.

'You again?' she said and smiled.

'Hi Nicola.'

'So, smoke this time, huh?' she asked. Grace nodded.

'I just need to clip this onto your finger to check your oxygen levels.' She waited a few seconds before checking the screen on the device. 'Okay, so it's not too bad, but it could be better. We'll give you some oxygen and get you to hospital for a full check-up.'

'And Mum?' Grace asked as paramedics wheeled her mum's stretcher into a waiting ambulance.

'Don't worry, she'll be fine. She has a concussion from the bump to the head, but it probably saved her life. You inhaled more smoke than she did because you were struggling so hard against those handcuffs.' She gestured to Grace's wrists which each had a raw band of skin where the cuffs had been. 'We'll get those cleaned up and bandaged when you get to hospital too.'

A second paramedic wheeled a stretcher over to her and collapsed it so it lay flat on the ground. 'Okay, can you shuffle onto this for me, Grace?' he asked.

Grace did as she was asked, and the stretcher was immediately raised to full height and wheeled into an ambulance. When she was inside, the paramedic lowered a mask over her face.

'This is oxygen. It should get your levels back up so you'll feel less groggy. We'll keep it on until you get to hospital then we'll see how you're feeling.'

Grace closed her eyes as the oxygen flushed through her system, and she was soon fast asleep.

When Grace awoke, DS Gonzales was at her bedside.

His hair was messy, like he'd spent the night running his hands through it. His usually pristine suit jacket was in a crumpled heap on the floor next to her bed. When he noticed she was awake, relief washed over his face.

'I'm so sorry, Grace.'

'Mum?' Grace panicked, instantly thinking the worst.

'Oh, no, no. Your mum's fine. Sorry. I'll start again.' He wiped a hand down his face. 'I'm sorry I didn't believe you when you said Jonathan Bainbridge killed Olivia. And I'm sorry we let him do this.'

Grace nodded. She could understand why the

detective felt bad. She *had* told him it was Johnny who killed Liv *and* there was supposed to be a police car watching their house. DS Gonzales could sense her unasked question. 'It turns out, the officers who were on the evening shift were creatures of habit and always got coffee from a roadside coffee stall on their way to your house. Unfortunately, Johnny must have had them watched and spotted this. The owner of the truck was happy to add some sedative to their coffees when Johnny offered him a significant amount of money. Then, he made the call to your mum, deliberately making the line sound bad so he could pretend he was me. Once the sedative had taken effect, Johnny took one of the officer's uniforms and went to your house.'

'And …?' Grace asked.

DS Gonzales smiled for the first time since she'd awoken. 'We got him, Grace. Your neighbour, Mrs Peel, spotted him leaving your house in a hurry and thought it was odd. She called us straight away and a patrol car picked him up a couple of streets away. He's not saying anything, but the minute Frank May heard Bainbridge was in custody, he told us absolutely everything. Apparently, Jonathan Bainbridge killed Olivia Montague. He'd cut his hand badly and was in no fit state to bury the body, so he'd got Frank to do it for him, saying if he didn't, he'd tell the police Frank had killed Liv. Then, to guarantee Frank's silence, he took a photo of Frank burying the body. Frank had felt so guilty though, that he'd planted the rose bush that you'd found as a kind of gravestone. Once Johnny had shown him the photo, he realised he could never tell anyone what had happened.'

'Jonathan Bainbridge then held it over him for all these years. After all, why would an innocent man bury a young girl's body? He'd have been convicted of Liv's murder in a heartbeat. But there's no way Mr Bainbridge will be able to crawl out of this one, even with the best lawyers in the world.' DS Gonzales stood. 'And it's all thanks to you, Grace. You are a truly remarkable young lady.' He opened the door to leave then smiled back at her. 'I think there's someone here you'll want to see,' he said as he left.

As soon as he'd stepped out of the door, a nurse entered, pushing a wheelchair. Grace's mum was sitting in it, a big bandage wrapped around her head, but otherwise looking great.

'Mum!' Grace cried, gripping her mum's hand tightly once she'd been wheeled next to Grace's bed. 'How are you?'

'Don't worry about me. How are you?' her mum asked.

The nurse spoke then. 'I'll answer for both of you. Good news. The doctor has checked your stats and you'll both be free to go home later on today. But you'll need to take it easy. No more detecting, young lady.' She smiled before leaving them alone in the room together.

CHAPTER 36

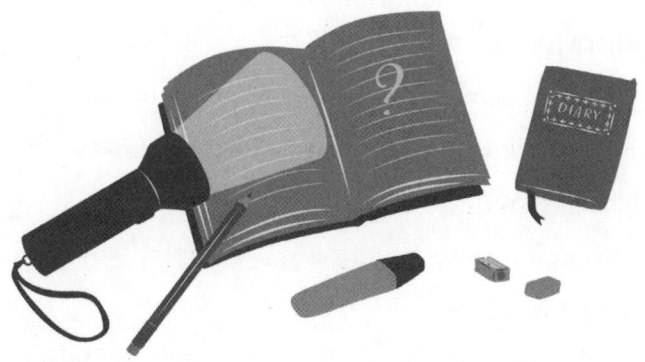

Ding-dong! *Tap! Tap! Tap!* went the door, the following Monday morning.

Grace grabbed her coat and ran down the stairs.

'Bye, Mum, I'm off to school!' she yelled, pulling open the door.

Suzy stood on the doorstep, her hair now a rainbow of colour from the roots to the tips.

Grace raised her eyebrows.

'D'you like it? I didn't think the acid green was really

my shade, so I thought I'd try something different,' Suzy offered as explanation.

'It suits you.' Grace smiled. 'Not sure what Beany will say though.'

'It's okay, I've come prepared!' Suzy rummaged in her bag and pulled out a woolly hat.

'Because that worked so well last time!' Grace pointed out.

'Second time lucky then!' Suzy quipped as they walked through the garden gate.

'Is it just me, or are you actually excited to go into school too?' Grace asked.

'Yeah. After the weirdness of the last few weeks and being cooped up at home, I just want a bit of normal. Plus, I get to find out if I got into coding club today!'

'They'd be crazy *not* to take you! When do you find out?'

'First break. I'm never going to be able to concentrate in French!' Suzy said.

They followed their usual route to school, and as they passed the florist shop, Scruff raced out of the door to greet them, his tail wagging furiously as he wound his body between Grace's legs.

'Hi there, Scruff,' she said, bending over to stroke him.

'Ah, there he is. I thought it was a bit peaceful in the shop!' Mrs Peel said, stepping outside. 'First day back at school, is it?'

'Yeah, it is ... um ... I haven't had a chance to thank you for everything you did for us, and ... well ... if you hadn't–,' Grace started.

Mrs Peel immediately dismissed her with a shrug. 'Don't be daft. Anyone would have done the same. I'm just glad you're both safe and those awful men have been arrested. Terrible to think what they did all those years ago.' She shook her head. 'Anyway, enough of that. You girls have a great first day back at school.' Mrs Peel smiled.

'Thanks,' Grace replied, checking her watch. 'Speaking of school, we'd better go. Don't want to be late on our first day back! See you later, Mrs P.' Mrs Peel waved then shepherded Scruff back into the shop, and the girls continued up the high street.

When they arrived at school, though, Jill and her gang were gathered right in front of the school doors.

Grace checked her watch again. Three minutes until the bell went for the start of the day.

'We can go round the back if you like?' Suzy said, noticing Grace's hesitation.

'No. After everything we've been through, I can handle Jill Blackburn.' She put her shoulders back, fixed her eyes straight ahead and strode towards the doors.

'Look who it is,' Jill sneered as they passed.

Grace and Suzy ignored her.

'Oh, so now you think you're all that, do you? Well, I don't think so. In fact, I heard you almost got your own mum killed while you were showing off pretending to be a detective!' Jill snorted and nudged Debbie, who stood next to her.

Debbie stepped away, a look of horror on her face.

Grace took one quick step towards Jill so she was nose to nose with her.

'Don't you *dare* talk about my mum. You don't

have a clue about what happened. I'm fed up with your snide comments and if I can take on a bully like Jonathan Bainbridge, I can deal with a nobody like you!' Grace said, looking levelly at Jill, whose mouth was hanging open.

'Yeah. Leave her alone,' came a voice to Grace's right. Debbie Gribbs had stepped away from Jill and now stood next to her.

'Yeah, Jill!' More of Jill's friends moved to stand next to Grace.

'Really? You all really want to do this? Well, you'd better watch your backs! I won't forget this!' Jill said.

'No, we'll watch each other's backs! That's what friends do, but you wouldn't know that, would you?' Grace bit back.

'Well, I don't need any of you losers!' Jill blustered, turning and hurrying through the school doors.

'Whoa, Grace, I never knew you had it in you!' Suzy hi-fived Grace.

'Nor did I!' Grace laughed.

The school bell rang to signal the start of the day,

and everyone made their way inside.

'See you at playtime?' Suzy asked.

'Yeah, I'll wait for you at the benches. Come find me after you've officially been accepted into coding!'

Suzy gave a quick salute before entering the first classroom on the left, and Grace carried on up the corridor towards geography. She stepped into the classroom and glanced around for a seat. She needn't have bothered.

'Over here, Grace! We've saved a seat for you.' Smiling, Debbie pointed at the seat next to her. On the other side of the empty desk was Abeer.

'Hey, Grace,' he greeted her as she sat down and was getting her books out of her bag. 'Glad to have you back.'

Grace smiled in return. 'Me too.'

Abeer leaned in closer, uncertainty and hope flickering in his eyes. 'Um, Grace?'

'Yes?'

'Have you … um … I mean … are you … that is … would you … um … like to go to the end of term ball with me?'

'Good morning, class. Today we're going to be continuing our work on glacial movement,' Mr Stewart said. A groan rippled across the class, but Grace didn't notice any of that.

'I'd love to,' she whispered. Debbie, clearly having overheard, poked her in the shoulder, giving her a double thumbs up.

'So, last lesson we learnt that lateral moraines ...'

Grace had other things to think about than glaciers. She was going to the ball with Abeer!

When the bell rang for the end of the lesson, Abeer waited while Grace packed up her things.

'Mind if I join you at break?' he asked.

'I'm meeting Suzy at the benches to find out whether she got into coding club, but I'm sure she won't mind you joining us.'

'Great. I'm just going to go and get a snack from

the canteen. Do you want anything?'

'No, thanks. I'm fine. See you outside,' Grace said, cringing inside. *Why didn't I offer to go with him? Now he's going to think I don't like him!* 'Actually ...' she started. But it was too late, Abeer was already stepping into the corridor.

Shaking her head at her own foolishness, she made her way to the benches.

It was a sunny morning but there was a definite chill in the air, so Grace chose one that was out of the shade. The sun instantly warmed her skin, and she glanced around her. Everything was so normal. It was like nothing had changed since last time she was in school, but she knew that wasn't true. *I've changed*, she thought. *It's only first break, and I've already stood up to Jill, made new friends and been asked to the ball.* She smiled to herself.

'What're you smiling at?' Suzy said as she and Abeer walked across the playground towards her. 'No, don't answer that. Abeer's already told me about the ball, so I can guess!' She grinned and Grace blushed furiously.

'Anyway, enough about you. Let's talk about me and coding club!' Suzy flung herself next to Grace on the bench.

'How'd it go?'

'Well, I didn't get in.'

'What!'

'Hang on, I've not finished! Paul, the one who runs the club, said my application was really strong, but they'd decided to give the place to Bobby.' She turned to Abeer. 'Bobby's entry was a robot that could navigate through a maze. Not bad, but I could do that in primary school.' She shrugged. 'Anyway, one of the other members, Tommy, said he'd heard that I'd rescued you using Morse code, and that if I could be that resourceful then I deserved a place in the club. You should have seen Paul's face!'

'So …?' Grace prompted, desperate to hear what happened.

'So, the other members got in a huddle to discuss if I could join or not and I overheard Paul say *girl* a lot; I think he might have a problem with girls. Long story short, Paul changed his mind and I'm in! The first girl in coding club!'

Grace squealed, hugging Suzy.

'I knew you could do it!'

'Well done, Suzy.' Abeer smiled, standing up. 'Right, I've got physics next, which is across the other side of the school, so I'd better head off.' He turned to Grace. 'See you at lunch?'

She nodded, grinning.

'Shall we head off too?' she asked Suzy.

'Yeah, why not.'

They stood up and made their way across the playground towards the school building. Away from the shelter of the benches, a chill wind made Grace shiver. As she pulled on her coat, she frowned.

Suzy looked over, concern etched on her face. 'What's the matter? It's not another vision, is it?'

'No. Nothing like that. It just feels … different somehow. It feels … normal.' Grace smiled wistfully, remembering the moment she'd heard that Liv had been returned to her family, who were holding a special burial service the following weekend.

'Well, I'm glad to hear it. Especially as I need a new school bag and you need a dress for the ball. I noticed someone has taken over that charity shop and it's reopened. They had some nice stuff in there when we bought your coat. Shall we take a look on the way home …?'

THE END

SARAH WYNNE

Sarah Wynne is from Chester in the northwest of England and lives with her husband, son and their little white ball of chaos, Daisy the dog. She spent over 10 years working as a primary teaching assistant but now writes full-time and provides editorial services to writers of children's fiction. When she's not writing, she'll usually be found with her nose in a middle grade book (or researching which book to read next or talking about books!).

LAURA BARRETT

Laura Barrett is an illustrator based in South London, specialising in intricate silhouette illustrations and decorative monochrome patterns. Her clients include the BBC, John Lewis, Marks & Spencer, Taschen and Penguin Random House. Laura creates artwork for design and publishing: illustrating packaging, children's picture books and book covers for all ages. Her illustrated books include *The Snow Queen*, *The Little Mermaid*, *The Nativity* and the *Fairy Tale Revolution* series.

Photo © Tom Skipp